D0454804

WILLIAM J. BAUSCH

——MORE——

TELLING
STORIES
COMPELLING
STORIES

TWENTY-THIRD PUBLICATIONS

Mystic, Connecticut 06355

Also by William J. Bausch:

Timely Homilies
Telling Stories, Compelling Stories
Storytelling: Imagination and Faith
Pilgrim Church
Becoming a Man
A New Look At the Sacraments
While You Were Gone
The Total Parish Manual
Storytelling the Word
The Parish of the Next Millennium
A World of Stories for Preachers and Teachers
Catholics in Crisis?
The Yellow Brick Road
The Word In and Out of Season
Brave New Church
The Best of Bausch CD-Rom

Fourth printing 2000

Twenty-Third Publications/Bayard
185 Willow Street
P.O. Box 180
Mystic, CT 06355
(860) 536-2611
(800) 321-0411

ISBN:0-89622-534-8
Library of Congress Catalog Card Number: 92-60889
Printed in the U.S.A.

Preface

"All this Jesus said to the crowd in parables. Indeed, he said nothing to them without parables." Thus St. Matthew's testimony (13:34), whose own infancy narratives show him to be no mean storyteller himself. Come to think of it, there are no lectures recorded from the mouth of Jesus (or pen: he wrote nothing), except those long discourses in that strange last gospel. Jesus obviously was a natural storyteller and those who followed him picked up the habit. True, there were philosophical ruminations from St. Paul on, but the real work of spreading the Good News fell to accounts of Jesus, his disciples, and a whole array of saints. Legends, tales, epics, and myths were the embodiments of deep truths. Stories told of how people actually *lived* the gospel. To this day who can forget Jesus as Francis Thompson's "Hound of Heaven," or Francis of Assisi reasoning with the wolf of Gubbio? Who was not tingled to hear Robert Bolt's dialogue between Sir Thomas More and Henry VIII, the former asking the latter why he needed his support when he had everyone else's, and Henry answering, "Because you are honest...There are those like Norfolk who follow me because I wear the crown, and there are those like Master Cromwell who follow me because they are jackals with sharp teeth and I am their lion, and there is a mass that follows me because it follows anything that moves—*and there is you.*" Who does not see Christ in the life story of a Dorothy Day or Archbishop Romero?

The gospel has always been best served by stories which, after all, came first and then only later the philosophizing, the necessary categories, the systematic theologies. So this volume entitled *More Telling Stories, Compelling Stories* is in the tradition of the ancient Christian enterprise: taking the truths and enfleshing them in life: desperate, riotous, mysterious, noble, grace-racked life as witnessed in men and women of all ages. Sometimes, of course, it happens that the story obscures the gospel, gets in its way. Sometimes it illumines a point, and sometimes it does what a story is supposed to do: leave a lingering aura floating in the mind and imagination, suggesting possibilities of grace and conversion.

So, then, to the twofold aim of this book. The first is spiritual reading. The book's intent is to offer these thirty-three pieces as reflections for the Christian life for the 1990s. They can be privately read piecemeal on a now-and-then basis. They can be used for prayer or discussion groups. They are relatively short and can give a focus to our lives and help us place these stories and our stories into the greater story of God's unconditional love.

The second aim of this book is to offer what master homilist Walter Burghardt, S.J., calls "the homiletic hint." That is, these thirty-three reflections are in homily format and to this extent they attempt to be suggestions on how to take the individual stories collected in books and homily services for preachers and teachers and weave them into the text of a particular Sunday. Which is why I have given the Scripture reference under each homily title and a lectionary reference at the end of this book. That is also why these pieces have a pastoral bias. Thus the stories used are meant to be points of scriptural focus and interpretation, and mostly, points of challenge and inspiration. Some stories, as we would expect, are more successful than others in doing this, and some homilies more superficial than others. Some do justice to the sacred word and others, alas, unwittingly subvert it. We can't always succeed.

Not all selections here will be to everyone's taste, expectations, or mood, but I hope there are enough of them to make for pleasing spiritual reading for the general population and a help to preachers. It's good to remember that these words were first spoken, and so there is absent in the printed word the gesture, the voice inflection, and that wonderful, mysterious rapport with one's fellow worshippers that ebbs and flows impact and emotion and whose body language and facial expression are one's greatest critics. What is missing is caught in that old story of the church cleaning woman coming upon the preacher's notes left in the pulpit. On the margin of the typewritten text is scrawled in his hand, "Argument weak here, yell like hell!" So the "yelling" is not here, and that's too bad. Still, I've included some personal notes and credits at the end that may supply some of that yelling.

Also included at the end of this volume are Lectionary References not only for the present volume of homilies, but for my two earlier books of homilies as well: *Timely Homilies* and *Telling Stories, Compelling Stories.*

I am indebted to many sources and insights, many of which are lost to memory, and to casual reading, but the ones I've remembered I have acknowledged in the endnotes. I am also indebted to Jerry DiSalvo who recorded these homilies and Gloria Ziemienski who transcribed them. And to the People of God at St. Mary's who tolerated them.

Chuck Anderson

In Memoriam

Since life is but a play,
we are none of us kings or cardinals or poor men in reality;
we are all of us mere children of our Father.

R.H. Benson

and for his father, Anthony Anderson, who cared.

Contents

Preface   v

1   Decide (Mark 9:38-43)   1

2   Sowing the Seed (Mark 4:26-34)   2

3   Anger (John 2:13-25)   11

4   Coming and Going (John 6:60-69)   15

5   The Weeping Christ (Mark 1:12-15)   21

6   Forgiveness (John 20:19-31)   26

7   Rejoice Sunday (Philippians 4:4-7)   32

8   Advertising for God (John 3:14-21)   38

9   The Failed Parent (1 Samuel 2:12-17)   44

10   Returning (Isaiah 55:6-9)   50

11   Baptism: The Crisis of Identity (Mark 1:7-11)   55

12   The Scribe (Mark 12:28-34)   61

13   Slouching Toward Bethlehem (Matthew 2:1-12)   66

14   The Radical Gospel (Matthew 25:31-46)   72

15 Stewardship (Mark 12:38-44)   78

16 Love of Self (Mark 12:28-34)   83

17 The Mother-in-Law's Restoration (Mark 1:29-39) 89

18 Decision Time (John 12:20-33)   94

19 Cross, Crown, and Commitment (Mark 10:35-45) 98

20 The Environmental Sabbath (Matthew 6:25-29)   104

21 The Desert Experience (Luke 3:1-6)   110

22 Lambs of God (John 1:29-34)   115

23 The Persistent Question (Luke 3:7-14)   120

24 The Visit (Luke 1:39-55)   125

25 Christmas Passion (Luke 2:1-14)   130

26 Who Is That? (John 15:1-8; Acts 8:26-40)   134

27 A Homily for a
      Long Time Dying (Mark 15:33-39;16:1-6)   139

28 Homily for a Cancer Victim (John 11:32-45)   143

29 A Time to Remember (Sirach 3:2-6;12-14)   148

30   Knowing the Enemy by Name (John 10:11-18)   152

31   The Surprises of the Pentecost (Acts 2:1-11)   156

32   The Call (Isaiah 6:1-2, 3-8; Luke 5:1-11)   161

33   Seven Beauties: An Entertainment   166

Notes   174

Lectionary References   178

   From:
     More Telling Stories, Compelling Stories   178

     Timely Homilies   181

     Telling Stories, Compelling Stories   184

1

✝

Decide

(Mark 9:38-43)

Some friends who went deer hunting separated into pairs for the day. And that night one hunter returned alone, staggering under an eight-point buck. "Where's Harry?" asked another hunter. "Oh, he fainted a couple of miles up on the trail," Harry's partner answered. "And you left him lying there all alone and carried the deer back?" "A tough call," said the hunter, "but I figure no one's going to steal Harry."

And that story is cousin to the old exclamation, "If I've told you once, I've told you a million times not to exaggerate!"

It's what we call hyperbole, using extravagant language to get a point across. I introduce the story and mention the use of hyperbole because, as you heard in the gospel this morning, you were subjected to such outrageous, terrible sounding things as plucking out eyes and cutting off arms in order to get to heaven. But we have to recognize that Jesus is using hyperbole here, severely exaggerated speech to make a point. Although it always makes me wonder about those who read the Bible literally. What do they do when they come to this passage? Obviously they make some adjustment. because I haven't seen too many one-eyed or one-armed Fundamentalists around.

Anyway, the basic message beneath this hand-lopping and eye-plucking is radical decision. That's what the bottom line is. A few weeks ago we had Billy Graham's Crusade in New York, and there and wherever he goes he gives his audience this final challenge: "Decide! Cut away anything that prevents you from a radical decision for Jesus Christ! Decide for Christ!" That is pretty much this morning's gospel message.

What are we to decide? To discover the answer we turn to a very famous picture that you've probably seen reproduced many times: the picture of Jesus standing outside a door overgrown with ivy. There's no knocker, no handle on the outside. The idea is that Jesus stands there and knocks but there's no way for him to enter unless someone on the other side of the door decides to open it and let him in. It's called "The Light of the World" and it's in St. Paul's Cathedral in London.

Those of you who have been to London know that St. Paul's has for a long time been situated in a very busy, commercialized area with heavy traffic. The result is that the picture got quite dirty. And so the Cathedral staff sent it to one of those places that restores art pieces. But when the restorers took the picture out of its frame to clean it, they saw something no one was intended to see. On the bottom, underneath the molding, the artist had written the words, "Forgive me, Lord Jesus, that I kept you waiting so long!"

The artist had known about Jesus and he had painted him on the other side of that door. He just regretted that he took so long to decide to answer and open up to him. Again, it's the same gospel message: it's time for radical decision. What decision? It's time to open the door to Jesus once and for all. And, like it or not, we must decide not just to open one door, but three: the door to the past, the door to the present, and the door to the future.

First, to open the door to the past is to face the reality that "what is done is done." That's it. What we did, you and I, the hurtful things, the heart-breaking things, the arrogant things, the unjust things—they're done and we can't undo them. The only way we can deal with past hurts and sins that haunt us is to open the door to Jesus. The name that tradition has for this opening is forgiveness.

There is a couple in one of Thomas Hardy's novels who had a daughter named Elizabeth, and Elizabeth died. And they agreed, this couple, that if they ever had another child and if that child turned out to be a girl, they would name her Elizabeth. And so they did have another child and it turned out to be a little girl and they did name her Elizabeth. But it didn't help. They realized that they could have had fifty daughters and named every one of them Elizabeth and they would *still* miss Elizabeth. Some things in life you don't fix. You have to swallow that and accept it.

There are some things that you and I don't fix: a death, a divorce, a hurt, a stupidity, a betrayal, an infidelity. They're there. The only response to these is forgiveness. To decide to open the door to Jesus Christ-of-the-past is simply to go to Jesus and ask for forgiveness, and that's it. And you move on to the future. We cannot undo what's been done, regret it though we might. We can only submit it to the unconditional love of Jesus who can absorb all things.

The alternative is to keep that door closed. And people do that. And Jesus—the compassionate Jesus—is out there knocking, but if we don't open it we wallow in our guilt and recriminations and contract our lives. Some things in life you cannot fix; they can only be forgiven. That's what the gospel is about. It urges, "Make your radical decision about the past; namely, cut it off, pluck it out. Open the door of the past to Jesus. Ask forgiveness, hand the past over to him, and slam the door shut."

Secondly, we must decide to open the door to the present and that means we ask ourselves, "What's going on in my life right now? What has to be cut off? What has to be plucked out if I am to be whole? What has to be put in perspective?"

I remember years ago a missionary friend of mine telling me

of his ordeal as a missionary in China. At that time (it hasn't improved that much) he and a family—a mother, father, and two children—were under house arrest. They had been under house arrest living somewhat comfortably for years. Well, one day a soldier came in and said, "You can all return to America. But you may take only two hundred pounds with you, no more, no less."

Well, they had been there for years, as I said. Two hundred pounds! So they got the scales and the family arguments started with the husband, wife, and the two children. "Must have this vase, must have this typewriter; it's almost brand new. Must have these books. Must have this, must have that." And so they weighed everything and took it off the scale. Weighed it and took it off, until, finally, right on the dot, they got two hundred pounds.

The soldier came the next day and asked, "Ready to go?" They said yes. He said, "Did you weigh everything?" They said yes. "Did you weigh the kids?" "No, we didn't." "Weigh the kids," he said. And in a moment, off went the typewriter, off went the books, off went the vase into the trash. The trash. The things that clutter our lives and separate us—into the trash. "Cut it off, pluck it out!" The time has come to decide to put things in perspective. That's the moment you open the door of the present to Jesus.

Last week I met a woman up by the parish house and I was kidding with her. I said, "What are you doing up here?" She said, "I've come to see Sister Pat for a massage." Sr. Pat Reynolds does healing and touch massage and teaches others how to do it. So, I kidded, "A massage, huh?" And suddenly she turned serious and said something that hit me in the gut. She said softly, "I live alone, and no one ever touches me."

And I thought about that. No one ever touches her. In effect she is paying someone to touch her, not with exploitation, not with violence, not with abuse, but with healing tenderness and affection. That must be a sore temptation for many people, since so many of us go off in different directions and so many of us widen the gaps between us with accumulations, schedules, activities, and self-fulfilling careers. Some people who live in the same house are not very often touched. Sometimes they have to pay someone to touch them. And the gospel comes back and shouts, "Cut it off! Pluck it out! If there are things between you and your loved ones that prevent you from touching as you should touch one another—make your decision. Open the door to the present moment."

The final door to open is the door to the future. This simply means to give yourself over to Christ. This is the Christ who said, "Come to me all of you who labor and are heavily burdened and I will refresh you." This is the Christ who said, "How often I would gather you as a mother hen gathers her chicks but you would not." This is the Jesus who says, "I am the way and the truth and the life."

Decide. Decide what you have to cut off and pluck out to open these three doors. And the next time you hear this rather upsetting gospel and remark to yourself, "My God, this sounds so gross and so awful!" just remember that this is Jesus' exaggerated way of saying, "Decide!" Decide what has to be chucked out of your lives in order to be free. Jesus stands at the door and knocks. With the artist we cry, "Forgive me, Lord Jesus, that I kept you waiting so long!"

So open the door of your past. There is forgiveness. Open the door to your present and take a look at all the unnecessary and divisive things you've got on the scales, and trash them. There is renewal. And open the door to the future. Hand over your life. There is promise. On the other side of all these doors stands the most unconditional Lover you'll ever meet.

"Behold," says that Lover, "I stand at the door and knock. Will you open up?"

This gospel, in its own violent way, demands a decision.

2

✝

Sowing the Seed

(Mark 4:26-34)

Let me tell you about Josephine. Josephine was only a little girl when her family moved to California. She was in the third grade and every day the bus would pick her up, like it did all the other kids, and drop her off. In her case, when the bus came back from school in the afternoon, her brother was waiting for her by the fence that surrounded the house. He was a year or so older than Josephine but he didn't go to school.

Some of the other students on the bus used to look for him and when they saw him they would laugh. They laughed at him because somehow they recognized that he was different. He looked and acted differently from the other kids. They didn't know why, and the kids on the bus didn't understand, so they laughed. They would wave to him and sometimes they would call out to him and he in turn would wave back to them only to make them laugh more.

But when Josephine got off the bus her brother would jump up and run to meet her. And to the other students' surprise, Josephine didn't seem at all embarrassed, though she knew behind her the kids on the bus were having a great time. She would greet her brother and hug him, and often she would just drop her books on the ground and throw both arms around her brother. And then, hand in hand, the two of them would march into the house.

Josephine was only a little girl, of course, but she had learned a very human lesson of love. And it took time—the rest of the school year, as a matter of fact—for the others to learn, but toward the end the other students gradually seemed to understand a bit more and their mocking behavior began to subside. Obviously some of the students' parents had heard about this and had spoken to their children. And then some of the other more perceptive children felt that somehow it was not right to be mocking this kid, and their example affected some of the others. Therefore they began to show a little kindness and compassion.

When anyone would ask Josephine about her brother, Josephine would simply say that her brother was retarded and would never be like the other kids, but he was her brother and she loved him. Later on, even a couple of the girls would come over and play at the house and they got to know Jimmy and would play with him as well. The children on the bus would still wave at Jimmy but this time it wasn't in mockery; it was with a little more gentle kindness and he would wave back.

And Josephine rode that bus for many years until finally her family moved away. But the image of those daily visits of Josephine embracing her brother and the evolving reaction of the kids on the bus remained in the memories of those students for a long time. Else you would not have heard this story which was told to me by a now fifty-year-old woman who was one of those students.

So the question now is this: Do you suppose that the remembrance of little Josephine and her brother Jimmy in any way influenced those school children, now grown to adulthood, to make them a tad more sensitive and compassionate? And what have they taught *their* children?

Let me tell you about Leon. Leon was a young man, a lad, really, growing up in Poland during the Second World War. Leon and his family were Jews. He had seen his parents and his other relatives and friends killed or hauled off to the concentration camps by the Nazis. Little Leon fled to a nearby farm and hid there. Still, as we said, he was only a boy and could not fend for himself. Somewhere along the line he had to reveal himself or he would die. And so one day he introduced himself to the farmer. The farmer and his wife happened to be very sensitive people, very good Catholics, and they hid Leon for years. They fed him and clothed him and took care of him even though, had they been caught doing so, they would have been instantly executed.

Well, after the war Leon grew up and moved to the United States. He went to school, was a brilliant student, and became a rabbi. To this day, Leon, as an older man now, tells his story of his childhood and the people who saved him and shares with his Jewish friends his great appreciation and empathy for the Catholic church because those Catholics of long ago were so good and gracious to him. And what happened to him so long ago operates every day in an ongoing ecumenical reach-out.

If you go to Europe this summer and visit the famous cathedrals, you will find that they are crowded. But unfortunately they are not crowded with worshippers; they are crowded with tourists. In many parts of Europe Catholicism has become a museum relic like the Coliseum. Only seven percent of the French and fifteen percent of the Italians practice their faith. Although most call themselves Catholic, they've abandoned their Catholic heritage.

But, on the other hand, if you go a few miles outside of Paris, you will come upon a community called L'Arche, founded by Jean Vanier. The L'Arche community is a community of retarded adults and the people who care for them and live with them and worship with them. L'Arche has branches all over the world, including foundations in this country. But what is significant is how many young people, in their twenties and early thirties, who could be cutting it big in the financial and corporate world, give months and years of their lives to live with these retarded adults to pray with them, live with them, and minister to them. And then they return to their world with powerful memories.

Several miles away in pagan France is the ecumenical community of Taizé, founded by the still-living and charismatic Brother Roger. The community is a combination of Catholics and Protestants and Orthodox, monks and young lay people, who take the vows of poverty, chastity, and obedience. They open their community to the world and share the worship and word of God with all who come. What is amazing, even spectacular, is the tens of thousands of young people who every summer flock with their knapsacks and meager belongings to Taizé to hear the word of God, find peace, worship, and be drawn to the holiness and lifestyles of the monks. Young people from countries that hate each other find common ground listening to the gospel of Jesus and seeing it lived. They are never the same after the visit.

One more example. In Rome right now there's a community called St. Igidio. If you were to visit it you would think you had stumbled on a young people's concert. Thousands of young people come to pray and minister to the poor and the sick and the homeless of Rome. Very frequently they are joined in prayer by a fellow pilgrim: Pope John Paul II. And they return home bearing new life.

And when I see such thousands of young people so hungry for the Word of God, so attracted to common decency and prayer, so enthralled by a sense of community, sharing, and service, I have to think how many of them are there because this is the first seeding of their lives. They are there searching for the lost seeds they never received when young, impressionable, and receptive. They are enchanted by what should be commonplace in their lives. Still, I thank God they *do* get seeded and life is never the same.

Why do I mention these things? I mention them because, as you listened to the Word of God today, you notice it is precisely about these things that the gospel speaks. What did Jesus say? He said the reign of God, that is, the actions and presence of God, is what? It is like a seed. You hardly know it's there. It's very tiny. It's imperceptible. But it's there and it grows nevertheless.

Half a century ago, don't you think the kids of Josephine's bus received the tiniest of seeds? So much so that you have a bus load of adults, now in their fifties, who are compassionate and sensitive to those who are different. Don't you think that thirty or forty years ago a seed was planted in a little Jewish boy who is now an ecumenically-minded rabbi in New York? Don't you think that the seeds planted at L'Arche, Taizé, or St. Igidio will sprout into deeds that will make a difference? *That's* what life is about, what the reign of God is about.

The reign of God is like a seed. That seed is the kindness we do, the worship we share in, the conversation around the dinner table, the soup to the sick neighbor, the decisions to put the family first. The seed is being sensitive to minorities, to restrict television in order to stem the flow of consumerism to your children's souls. The seed is making your children bring back the little things they've stolen, and apologize. The seed is having them catch you at prayer. The seed is your being here.

I like the seed symbol, mostly, I guess, because it fits me. I can handle a seed. We seldom have the opportunity, or even the courage, to do the big things, the really big, heroic things. But every day we all have the opportunity to do the small ones that display our values and the values of Jesus; values, perhaps, small as a seed, but seeds that will bear fruit thirty, forty, fifty years from now. Josephine, Leon's befrienders, Jean Vanier, Brother Roger—all are spiritual Johnny Appleseeds.

And this is what this gospel calls *us* to be.

3

+

Anger

(John 2:13-25)

One man is talking to another. "My wife and I," he exclaims, "got angry last night and we had a fight." His friend asked him, "How did it end up?" "How did it end up? Why she came crawling to me on her hands and knees!" "What did she say?" "She said, 'Come out from under that bed, you coward!'"

That's a veteran vaudeville story. If you want an updated version: the wife called her husband deliriously on the phone. She could hardly catch her breath from the excitement. "Harry," she cried, "I won the lottery! I won the lottery! Pack your clothes!" "Great!" said Harry. "Summer or winter?" "All of them," she said. " I want you out of the house by six!"

Thus anger, hostile and sarcastic—and both different from the anger Jesus displayed in today's gospel. And to appreciate that, we have to note several things. One, which is rather incidental, is to observe that an angry Jesus is not our customary image of him. Our usual image that is always found in poor art and sculpture is that of a wan, androgynous, casual Jesus. And here we have a rather strong, angry, and violent Jesus who makes a whip and drives animals and people out of the Temple grounds. This picture is a good antidote to sentimentality.

Two, it is worth noting as you listen to this familiar story, is that in fact the Temple transactions were perfectly legal. Since the Jews were in occupied territory they had to use the money of the occupiers, the Roman coin, which, you recall from another gospel incident, carried Caesar's image on it. Such a blasphemous image would violate the Mosaic law and so when they went to the Temple—their preserve and territory—they had to exchange the hated coin with its image for their own shekel. And they also had to buy ritualistically clean animals. So it was a perfectly legal Temple arrangement, not to mention that this arrangement was a monopoly that made a good profit for the Temple and the dealers themselves.

But this legal arrangement exploited the poor. It was what we call today "structural injustice"; that is, the injustice, though legal, is built right into the system. Much like abortion is legal, but it's an injustice built into its very structure. It was this that got Jesus angry, this form of exploitation and oppression of the poor. But his anger went deeper in two ways. First, it was aimed at the practice that the Temple itself, organized religion, was implicated in. Jesus was fundamentally attacking worship, worship without pity, works without mercy. He was attacking religion, religion without substance, ritual without justice. Second, he was attacking others' lack of anger at this daily, routine, commonplace injustice. Had no one noticed? Was no one scandalized? Was no one saddened? Had all become dulled? It's enough to make one who loves God angry, very angry.

So Jesus showed anger, the kind of anger that reverberates throughout the ages. And it rolls down to us as a Jesus angry with our worship that leaves us unchanged and our world unchanged. A Jesus angry at our domestication of the Good News. A Jesus angry at people making God an undemanding, indifferent, and benign granddaddy, instead of the Abba Father who absolutely will not forgive us unless we forgive our brother and sister from our hearts. A Jesus who asks in effect why *we* are not angry at certain things. Indeed, we confirm the old truism that the opposite of love is not hate; it is indifference.

If it is true that we are physically what we eat, it is equally true that we are morally what we get angry at. Think of that. What riles us? Not just people cutting us off at the parking lot; but, deep down, what makes us angry? Or what doesn't—and should? Does poverty make us angry, the grossly unequal spread of wealth? Does Homelessness? Abortion? Exploitation of the poor? Discrimination? Infidelity? Racism? What will anger us in the name of the Lord? What will force us to action? When will our faith live?

It was a Sunday morning in South America, in a little chapel on the border of Venezuela and Colombia. As Mass was beginning a not uncommon occurrence happened: a band of guerillas armed with machine guns came out of the jungle and crashed and banged their way into the chapel. The priest and the congregation were totally horrified and afraid. They dragged the priest outside to be executed. Then the leader of the guerillas came back into the chapel and demanded, "Anyone else who believes in this God stuff, come forward!" Everyone was petrified. They stood frozen. There was a long silence.

Finally, one man came forward and stood in front of the guerilla chief and said simply, "I love Jesus." And he was roughly tossed to the soldiers and also taken out to be executed. And several other Christians came forward saying the same thing and they too were driven outside. Then the sound of machine gun fire. When there were no more people left willing to identify themselves as Christians, the guerilla chief returned inside and told the remaining congregation to get out. "You have no right to be here!" And with that he herded them out of the chapel where they were astonished to see their pastor and those others standing there.

The priest and those people were ordered to go back into the chapel to continue the service while the others were angrily warned to stay out "until," said the guerilla chief, "you have the courage to stand up for your beliefs!" And with that the guerillas disappeared into the jungle.

A powerful story. Is it too much to project Jesus into it? Jesus is the guerilla chief, full of anger, who challenges us, "Do you believe in this stuff? Do you act on it? When you rouse yourself and get angry and passionate enough for the gospel, when you hunger and thirst after justice, when you put yourself on the line, then you're worthy to continue your worship. Otherwise you have no right to be here." Strong stuff.

We can also now appreciate that rather cryptic remark at the end of today's gospel when the Temple leaders demand to know who gave Jesus authority to get so angry and do what he did. Jesus replies, "Destroy this temple"—pointing to himself—"and in three days it will be raised up." The point they missed is that the crucifixion was the sign of how seriously Jesus took religion. He could get so angry at evil that evil got angry at him and attempted to destroy him. If evil doesn't persecute you, you're its friend. Jesus' cross signifies righteous anger and the cost of it. It's the kind of righteous anger that leads people to confront indifference wherever it is. In the Temple. Even in church.

4

+

Coming and Going

(John 6:60-69)

The question in this morning's gospel is one that every generation of believers has had to face at one time or another: "Will you also go away?" Some, in fact, have gone away. Left the church. I suspect that there are very few of us here who do not know of someone, even members of our own family, who has gone away. Some have gone loudly and publicly, and others have gone quietly and privately, and still others have just drifted or faded away.

Some have found the message of Jesus too hard to take, too unrealistic. You know, the tone of his teaching about chastity and fidelity. His words about meekness, forgiveness, and honesty—concepts that sound good but don't hold up too well in the world today. Some have found Jesus' message beautiful, compelling, and lofty but could find no one who practiced it. Some like Jesus but can't stand his church. Some personally like the disciples but can't abide the church's leadership. Some wanted a church of all saints, and got a pack of sinners instead. Some wanted a church of sinners—more congenial—and got bothered by the saints. Some liked the rules, since they brought security; you knew where you stood: black was black, white was white, vice was vice, and virtue was virtue. Some hated the rules, since they brought imprisonment and moral brainwashing.

And some have been attracted away from the church by false gods. Some people—former church members included—gave their hearts and souls to communism before its spectacular fall. This communism, as we know, did not bring salvation; rather, in the annals of human history it imprisoned, tortured, deprived, and killed more human beings than any other system on earth. Others have found the gods of materialism and consumerism mightily attractive—until, like Dorian Gray, they exact their price. Others have slipped into the cracks of divorce and remarriage, and others have been lured by the securities of fundamentalism. Whatever the reason, they left the church. "Will you also go away?" They have said "yes," or at least have allowed "yes" to happen.

But there are others, such as ourselves, who have responded to Jesus' question with Peter's words: "To whom shall we go?" For all of its limitations, this is the church where we have touched God and God has touched us. Or, to put it another way, the question for us is not "Will you also go away?" but rather, "Why do you stay?" For some, that's easy to answer; for others, they find it harder to put an answer into words other than "I was born a Catholic." Anyway, I ask myself that question and find that, when you come down to it, the answer *is* hard to put into words. I suppose, if pressed, I could try to offer some lofty philosophical or theological reasons, but on reflection I think that, in the long run, stories and experience are the lived reasons why most of us really stay. And so I would like to share with you the stories of four people who are four reasons why I stay. You have, I am sure, your own private list, but here's a group that belongs to us all. One is an archbishop, another is a housewife, the other is a mystic, and the last is a professor.

As for the archbishop, most of you know by now that in

1977 Oscar Romero was a quiet and traditional cleric when he was consecrated archbishop of San Salvador. In fact, he was deemed so safe by the authorities that they used his very installation as bishop as an excuse for more government-sanctioned murders. This shook the archbishop deeply. He was even more troubled when some of his priests who lived among the poor people got to trust him enough to share with him the saying they had: "The church is where it always should have been: with the people, surrounded by wolves."

When one of these same priests was murdered by the government the archbishop delved more deeply into the gospel, met Christ in a most profound way for the first time, and soon was transformed from an amiable cleric to a forthright disciple of Jesus against injustice. And, like Jesus, he earned the hatred and fear of the establishment. The shadow of the cross began to cast itself over his life and ministry. But he was compelled by the gospel to speak out. And so it happened on March 24, 1980, Archbishop Romero celebrated Mass at the Chapel of Divine Providence in San Salvador. As he came to that part of the Mass that we all know so well, he lifted up the Host and said—as we shall say at this Mass—the ancient words, "This is my body, given for you. This is my blood shed for you." At that moment a rifle shot rang out, a bullet pierced his heart and he fell dead in the sanctuary. He became Eucharist. Like Jesus, he became a martyr for the truth, a prophet of justice, a man caught by the gospel, one who would not go away. I suppose in the course of history there have been unworthy, worldly, and profane archbishops, but *this* archbishop, who lived and died like Jesus, who is in *my* tradition, *my* church—he is the reason I stay.

Then there's the housewife. She tells her story. She says she was out shopping and came across a delightful gift shop. "I almost tiptoed into the gift shop," she says. "I saw hundreds of fragile items that were displayed on the glass shelves, and pausing to admire a one-of-a-kind sculpture of an English village, I strained to see as much detail without actually touching it. And suddenly a female voice behind me said, 'Please pick it up if you like.' I turned around and there was a woman who smiled and said, 'Don't worry; you can rely on our store policy.' She pointed to a small sign on a display case. It read: 'If you break it, please tell us so we can forgive you.'"

The housewife said she laughed and said to the saleswoman, "Now, that's what I call a novel approach in modern business." The saleswoman nodded and said, "Yes, since we put that sign up breakage hasn't really changed, but it's wonderful how much more comfortable everybody feels. In fact, it's made such a change in my own attitude that I took one home and my kids love it."

After she left the shop, the housewife mused to herself, "I guess it's human nature. There's something about knowing you'll be forgiven for a mistake that frees you to relax and enjoy yourself." And then she had a sudden thought: "It's like the forgiveness of God," she concluded. And she smiled to herself.

I suppose there are hundreds and thousands of housewives who shop daily and visit a million gift shops, but *this* housewife of my tradition resonates with an ordinary shopping event and hears the message of God's forgiveness. And she is why I stay.

The third person is a mystic, the medieval mystic, St. Catherine of Siena. She was asked by one of her nuns, "How can I pay God back for all of his goodness to me? How can I give back to God some glory for all of God's kind compassion, mercy, and generosity?" St. Catherine answered, "It won't do you any good to do any more penances. It won't do much good to build a great church. It won't do you much good to add more quiet time in prayer. But I'll tell you something you can do to really pay God back for the compassion God gives you. Find someone as unlovable as you are and give that person the kind of love that God has given you." I suppose that in the course of history there have been fraudulent, misguided, and ivory-towered mystics, but *this* mystic is genuine, sound, and practical, and she stands in my heritage and I in hers and she is why I stay.

And, finally, there is a professor in Boston, not in a religious, but in a very secular university. He died in 1987, the year I was taking a brief sabbatical at Boston College. He had the temerity to stand up in front of his students on the occasion of his retirement and deliver these lovely words. "When I was young, just starting out, I made a prayer to God. Over the years I would bring it out and pray it all over again many times, especially on important or significant occasions. Tonight is one of those occasions, perhaps one of the last ones in my life." And here he reached inside his coat pocket and drew out an old piece of paper, adjusted his glasses, and began to speak, not a speech, but a prayer as if prayed fresh for the first time.

"I'd like to be a flower in the garden of God. I'd like to take my chances in the wind and the rain, in the storm and sunshine. I'd like to be planted among a variety of species in the midst of an assortment of colors and sizes and shapes, and to grow among the lilies and the lilacs and the crocuses and chrysanthemums, the poppies and the pansies; and yes, even among the dandelions and the daisies. I want to be a part of that, an absolute riot of color and beauty.

"I pray God that I might last long enough to blossom. And then, Lord, early if you want to, late if you can, I want you to pick me. And if I must be alone in a solitary vase, I'll take it. I'd rather be in a bouquet. But could I be something beautiful, Lord, and placed on your table at someone else's covenantal moment?—when they're bringing their child, or when they're burying their beloved, or when they're sealing a vow? Could it be possible that someone would say, 'That reminds me of a flower I once saw, a Rose of Sharon, a Lily of the Valley, who was once picked by God and gave his life to add beauty and significance to the lives of others'?"

Then he put the paper down and spoke to the students: "My friends, God's love is there for all those who choose to seek God. Grace brings us victory over death and leads us to the eternal gifts of ultimate healing and salvation. My prayer for you this day is that you can begin to search with all your heart, soul, and mind for the things that are unseen so that you may find the strength and peace of God that enables us to live and then to die, knowing that life has been well lived in the service of God and the people of God. May we all live and die as flowers in the garden of God, giving glory to him in life, in death, and in resurrection."

I have known atheistic professors, agnostic professors, closet believer professors, but *this* professor with his courage to stand up and bear witness is the reason why I stay.

And so we have an archbishop, a housewife, a mystic, and a professor. And when someone asks me, "Will you also go away?" I respond, "What! and leave all these people? Not on your life. Like Peter, they have shown me who has the words of eternal life."

5

✦

The Weeping Christ

(Mark 1:12-15)

Once more we find ourselves in the course of our Christian pilgrimage at the first Sunday of Lent, the inaugural time for a communal forty-day journey of special intensity. And sometimes, in fact, most times, it helps us to have a rallying theme, a particular kind of focus to get us through these days with encouragement and purpose; that is to say, it helps us to have an overriding image that moves with us and compels us forward, an image that suggests both the journey and its goal. And so I would like to explore with you two items that might lead us to just such an image. The first item is a poem and the other a story. First, the poem.

It was written in England and there carries a reference to the industrial city of Birmingham, which is something akin to our Pittsburgh or any large American city. It goes like this:

When Jesus came to Golgotha,
They hanged him on a tree.
They drove great nails
Through hands and feet,
And made a Calvary.

They crowned him with a crown of thorns,
Red were his wounds and deep:
For those were crude and cruel days,
And human flesh was cheap.

When Jesus came to Birmingham
They simply passed him by.
They never hurt a hair of him,
They only let him die.

For men had grown more tender,
And they would not give him pain;
They only just passed down the street
And left him in the rain.

Still, Jesus cried, "Forgive them,
For they know not what they do."
And still it rained a winter rain
That drenched him through and through.

The crowds went home and left the streets,
Without a soul to see.
And Jesus crouched against the wall
And cried for Calvary.

Of course, the point of the poem is that the indifference of the people was worse than their active hostility when they nailed him to the cross. And so Jesus wept.

The story? That comes from Walter Wagerin who tells of his little son Matthew, a whirlwind of a lad, willful and determined. When Matthew decided to do something he just dashed headlong in and did what he wanted to do without too much thinking of the consequences. So one day, Walter relates, he went into his son's room and found him sitting on the bed with a whole stack of comic books around him. He said to Matthew, "Where did you get the comic books?" Matthew said, "I took them out of the library." "You took them out of the library?" "Yes." "You mean you *stole* them from the library?" "Yes." So the father called the librarian and said that he was going to march his son Matthew right down with the comic books and apologize and restore what he had stolen. He did precisely that and the librarian gave little Matthew a stern lecture about stealing.

Well, the following summer they vacationed at a small community in Vermont where there was a general store. When they returned home after the summer, at the beginning of the fall, the father went into Matthew's room and found a pile of comic books in his dresser drawer. And Matthew said, "I stole them from the store this summer." So the father took the comic books and he went into the den and he started a fire in the fireplace and he threw the comic books into the flames, and with each comic book that he threw into the flames, he reminded little Matthew of the seventh commandment, "Thou shalt not steal."

A year later, Matthew again stole some comic books, and this time his father told him that he was going to have to spank him. He brought him into the study and put him over his knee, and spanked him five times with his bare hand. Why five times? Because he felt that if he did any less he would be too soft and if he was really angry he might do too many, so he limited himself to five. He spanked Matthew and he sat him down, and he could see his son's head hanging; it was obvious that Matthew did not want to shed a tear in front of his father. The father understood that. And so not wanting to see little Matthew cry he said, "Matthew, I'm going to leave you alone for a while, but I'll be back in a few minutes." And after he stepped out of the room and closed the door behind him, the father himself began to cry and began to cry really hard. And he went into the bathroom and washed his face and went back into the study and talked to his little son Matthew.

Years later when Matthew was a teenager and he and his mother were driving back from a shopping trip, as often happens, they were reminiscing. And the reminiscence happened to come around to those early days when Matthew was a rascal stealing comic books. And Matthew said to his mother, "You know, after that incident with Dad, I really never stole anything again." And his mother commented, "I suppose the reason was because your father spanked you." "Oh, no," replied Matthew, "it was because when he stepped out of the room I could hear him crying."

That poem and this story, I suggest, might provide us with a deep image, a personal focus, when we prepare to move though Lent. The image I propose is simply Jesus Weeping.

In the gospels, you recall, Jesus overlooked the city of Jerusalem and wept. "Oh, Jerusalem, Jerusalem," he cried; "how often I would have gathered you as a mother hen gathers her chicks, but you would not." He wept too over his friend Lazarus, over his death, over what death did to his sisters and neighbors and that entire village. On the night before he died he said, "I no longer call you servants but friends," and when one of those friends betrayed him it's not hard to sense not only the pained voice but the tear in his eyes as he said, "Judas, do you betray the Son of Man with a kiss?"—the friendship kiss at that.

This weeping of Jesus stayed with the Christian community. Peter cried his tears basically because he could not stand Jesus'. The image got translated into popular piety recognized anywhere from the Dürer woodcuts where the thorn-crowned and sobbing Christ is sitting holding his head in his hands, to the First Friday devotions which told of the visions of St. Margaret Mary Alacoque who saw Jesus with his wounded heart complaining, "Behold the heart that has loved people so much and has received so little love in return." And he wept.

I suggest that this image of the Weeping Christ might be ours for the lenten journey. What we do for Lent, what we surrender, is not for its own sake, nor for our own self-improvement. What we do—the good deeds done, the prayers said, the sacrifices given—all have as their goal a deep and personal relationship with Jesus Christ. To know him with a burning desire, to love him with a burning passion. And that's why an image of Jesus is important. It places him at the center, and at the center as friend and lover. And the phenomenon of weeping tells us that Jesus is someone with feelings, someone who cares enough to be pained by what his friends do; who is highly susceptible, because of his love for us, to our betrayals that quite reduce him to tears.

He weeps over our version of stealing comic books; he doesn't like what it is making us become, in the hurt we're giving others. Like Walter, he cries, not from hatred of his son, but from love. So the Weeping Christ becomes our mantra, if you will, our mental image. If we contemplate the Weeping Christ long enough we will turn from our sins. It won't be because we fear the spanking. It will be because we can hear Jesus crying.

6

✝

Forgiveness

(John 20:19-31)

Carefully backing into a parking lot space, the driver of a big, heavy old Rolls Royce was angered when a teenager in a cool sports car zipped in and stole his place. Getting out of the car, the youth grinned and said, "You got to be young and quick to be able to do that, Pops." The older gent grinned too, and continued to back up his Rolls, crunching the tiny sports car into a total wreck. "And you have to be old and rich to be able to do *that*, Son," he said.

I share this story because it has a lot to do with the theme of today's liturgy, which is forgiveness. At first, we must admit, we are easily distracted by dealing only with the more appealing and exotic gospel story of Thomas, his doubt and dramatic reclamation. But when we are sidetracked too narrowly like this, we miss the whole impact of the combined three readings that tell us that the point of the second Sunday after Easter, and the first indication from Jesus of what his faith community would be about, was that it would be, above all, like himself, a reconciling community. In a word, the one who prayed for his persecutors' forgiveness as he hung on the cross left that legacy to his community as one of its most outstanding characteristics.

Forgiveness of those who have harmed us—who are harming us—then, is the hallmark of Christianity. The very message of Calvary itself and the first message of the Risen Christ is: "Receive the Holy Spirit. Whose sins you shall forgive, they are forgiven them." Such open forgiveness was, when you think of it, a profoundly shocking idea then, and is a profoundly shocking idea now. And yet, on those occasions when it has been put into practice, we recognize its authenticity.

Elsa Joseph was a Jewish woman who was cut off from both her children, both girls, during the Second World War. It was years later that she discovered that her daughters had been gassed at Auschwitz. A former concert violinist, Elsa responded to this tragic news by picking up her violin and going to play it in Germany. And there in the halls of the homeland of her children's murderers she played her violin and told her story that cried out to heaven for vengeance. But she did not seek vengeance. She spoke of the world's deep need for reconciliation and forgiveness, without which it was tearing itself apart.

"If I, a Jewish mother, can forgive what happened," she told her audiences not only in Germany, but in Northern Ireland, and in Lebanon and in Israel, "then why can you not sink your differences and be reconciled to one another?"

Then there is the Anglican Bishop Tafi, who, when he heard the news that his son, a university student at Teheran, had been waylaid and shot to death, forced himself to his knees and he prayed, "Father, forgive them; they know not what they do." Archbishop Oscar Romero, hearing rumors that the San Salvador death squads were out to get him, wrote that he pardoned and blessed his killers beforehand. An eyewitness reported that Father James Carney, an American priest in Honduras, who was murdered there, prayed for his murderers before they threw him out of a helicopter to his death below.

It is this radical concept of forgiving love, grounded in Jesus' witness, that sharply distinguishes such people as Elsa

Joseph, Bishop Tafi, Archbishop Oscar Romero, and Father James Carney from those other martyrs, the Kamikaze terrorists. Yes, both share one thing in common: they are prepared to die for a cause. But whereas the terrorist, in dying, adds to the violence of the world, hating and cursing what he has killed and encouraging others to do the same, the man or woman who responds to violence by begging God to have mercy on its perpetrators comes close to redeeming the world.

We may feel in our bones that such heroic forgiveness as we just mentioned is beyond us, and yet we recognize that when forgiveness is actually given and practiced, it speaks to the world's deepest needs. If the world is to be saved, the chain of evil and the vicious cycle of revenge have to be broken. It was Mohandas Gandhi, I think, who said that if you practice an eye for an eye and a tooth for a tooth, you're going to wind up with a universe of toothless and blind people.

An unknown woman in the Ravensbruck concentration camp wrote this little prayer and pinned it to the dead body of a little girl there. I'd like to share her prayer. "Oh, Lord," she wrote, "remember not only the men and women of good will, but also those of ill will. But do not remember all the sufferings they have inflicted on us. Remember rather the fruits we have bought, thanks to this suffering: our comradeship, our loyalty, our humility, our courage, our generosity; the greatness of heart that has grown out of all of this. And when they come to judgment, let all the fruits we have borne be their forgiveness."

Betsie Ten Boom, who died in the same concentration camp, steadfastly refused to hate the guards who beat her and eventually beat her to death. Her dying words are both simple and profound. Listen to what she said: "We must tell the people what we have learned here. We must tell them that there is no pit so deep that he is not deeper still." That is incredible: There is no pit so deep that Jesus is not deeper still. Calvary in the twentieth century!

For all of that, the injunction to forgive, the inner demand of being a Christian to forgive, there are people who cannot bring themselves to offer forgiveness. And there are people who cannot bring themselves to accept it. I think of a man that every once in a while I visit in jail. He should be there because he has committed a terrible murder. But he's so caught up in his own guilt that he cannot accept forgiveness, even from God. He feels there is no hope for himself either in this world or the next. He spends his time hugging his guilt to himself, thereby blocking out the forgiveness of the Christ who is on record for forgiving other murderers.

This man is light years away from another murderer in Dostoyevsky's great classic, *Crime and Punishment.* Here the murderer recognizes his guilt, his unworthiness, but offers them as the very reason for being open to mercy. He cries out in a famous passage from the book:

"You're right. I don't deserve any pity. I ought to be crucified. Crucified and not pitied. But he who takes pity on all men will also take pity on me. And he who understands all men and all things, he alone is judge. And he will judge all and will forgive them: the good and the bad, the wise and the meek. And when he has done with all of them, he will say unto us, 'Come forth, you also. Come forth, ye who are drunk. Come forth, ye who know no shame.' And we shall all come forth without being ashamed, and we will stand before him. And the wise will say, and the learned will say, 'Lord, why dost thou receive them?' And he will say unto them, 'I receive them, oh wise men, I receive them, oh learned men, because not one of them ever thought himself worthy of it.' And he will stretch out his arms to us, and we shall fall down before him, and we shall weep, and we shall understand all."

Forgiveness. There are probably very few of us here who have not been hurt or know people who have been hurt deeply. A spouse has walked out of our lives. Children have disappointed us. Parents have abused us. Friends have betrayed us. The company to which we gave so much devotion has fired us without notice, leaving us unemployed and bitter. We have been refused promotion. We have been treated unfairly. There's a host of deep and abiding hurts in the personal histories of most of us.

But forgiveness is hard, isn't it? To consciously break the vicious cycle of revenge is hard. Forgiveness, after all, is the deliberate decision to put up with an uneven score, and that rubs our American psyches the wrong way. To surrender a right to get even in a nation of Rambos with Uzi machine guns blasting enemy bodies all over the media is almost un-American. But the point is that we are not just anybody. We are a community that was born out of Calvary's forgiveness, called to be a reconciling community.

A wise man who knows what it means to forgive—his youngest son had been brutalized by a police officer—offers three somewhat earthy bits of practical advice that are worth sharing. He said, "I'm not very good at spiritual discipline, but after being called by a friend to practice what I preach, I sat alone in my study and made believe I was a priest in the confessional. I said out loud, 'Officer, in the name of God, I forgive you.' I felt kind of foolish at this creative hypocrisy, but it did get the juices of forgiveness going. I felt the caricature I had made of the officer change. Oh, a year later when that same cop drove past my house I had to go through the whole forgiveness process again. Forgiveness by fallible creatures is repetitious." That's real wisdom. For us weak creatures forgiveness indeed turns out to be a repetitious affair.

The second bit of wisdom he offers is this: "Don't forgive too fast." By that he doesn't mean to harbor lingering revenge. He means that we have to allow time for the hurt to surface, for the hatred to be visible and recognized and acknowledged to the point when perhaps we can say out loud, "I hate you." It is only when the hurt, the enemy, is out there and regurgitated that we can feel its full impact and come to terms with forgiveness. That's what our friend means by saying "Don't forgive too fast." Otherwise our forgiveness is too shallow. It hasn't grabbed sufficiently hold of the evil.

And finally he gives this delightful advice: "It's good to remember that when you pray for your enemies it doesn't automatically make them your friends. They are still your enemy. They're still out to get you. They still hate your guts." And he adds for emphasis: "They are still your enemies and you'd better guard against them because they might wallop you when you're down on your knees."

But that's their problem. Yours and mine is to enter into today's Scriptures, especially the gospel. And to remember that it's not a gospel of Jesus talking to priests; it is a gospel of Jesus talking to the entire community. His Easter gift is to breathe into that community the spirit of Calvary: "Receive its spirit. Whose sins you shall forgive they are forgiven." This is not only our mandate to continue the mission of Jesus. It turns out to be the condition of our own forgiveness, for we must remember that we were also commanded to pray thus to the Father, "Forgive us our trespasses *as* we forgive those who trespass against us."

7

+

Rejoice Sunday

(Philippians 4:4-7)

The man in the shadows waited pretty much until the family got all of its belongings into the car, checked everything, had the car loaded up, and pulled away for their summer's vacation. The man in the shadows waited until it was dark and then he went to the front door of the house and rang the bell. When there was no answer, this man, seasoned burglar that he was, had no trouble picking the lock and getting inside. As a precaution he called out into the darkness, "Is anybody home?" and he was stunned when he heard a voice reply, "I see you, and Jesus sees you."

Terrified, the burglar called out, "Who's there?" And again the voice came back, "I see you, and Jesus sees you." So the burglar switched on his flashlight toward the direction of the voice and was immediately relieved to see a caged parrot who recited once more, "I see you, and Jesus sees you." He laughed to himself and then went to the wall and threw on the wall switch. Then he saw it. Beneath the parrot's cage was a huge Doberman Pinscher. Then the parrot said, "Attack, Jesus, Attack!"

It's good to laugh out loud because as you attended to that second reading, you heard St. Paul start out by saying, "Rejoice! Have joy!" And even though there's a lot to be sad about—the possibility of war, recession, and a whole litany of troubles that daily press in on us human beings—we are nevertheless invited on this Third Sunday of Advent to laugh a little and rejoice. The Advent wreath itself with its four candles calls us to do just that, for there is that rose-colored candle we lit today, a mixture of the sadness of purple and the joy of white, which asks us to rejoice in the in-between time: the waiting of Advent and the promise of Christmas.

A photographic exhibit is making the rounds of the country these days; some of you may get to see it. It's called "Children in Photography: 150 Years." It's mostly black and white photos of children by famous photographers, and although there are sad photos of children who are hurt or deprived or weeping, by and large the photographs are of children laughing and rejoicing, children playing, children with their parents, children being whimsical, but, above all, children laughing. Printed notes give a little commentary on each of the photographs. The one beneath the children laughing is rather interesting and arresting. It says simply that when children laugh something breaks open in the universe. They're good words. When you and I hear a child spontaneously, fully, whimsically laugh, we have to smile. Something in the universe is indeed opened up. There is a certain joy.

And that's what we're asked to think about today. Forget the troubles and concentrate on the blessings, on joy. Joy is what? The welcome visit. The letter in the mailbox. The unexpected gift. The special dish we relish so much. The thoughtful child. The enthusiastic pet.

There was a couple who had lost their five-year-old daughter tragically to one of those childhood diseases. At the funeral they quietly said, "She brought us much joy." And I remember a taciturn old Irishman speaking of his son who was killed in the war. He simply said, "We had the joy of him."

But I think of all the joys in life, the one that is probably the deepest and most meaningful is the joy of liberation, a theme that is reflected in our Scriptures today, especially the liberation from bondage and fear. To be liberated from these two is indeed a cause for profound joy.

To catch just how deep that joy can be, listen to an article by a woman named Paula Dukes who asked her readers, in their imaginations, to put themselves back into an old, familiar biblical scene: the great Exodus of the Israelites from Egypt. They have at last been freed from their harsh taskmasters and at the point where her story begins the Israelites are going through the Red Sea with its terrifying walls of water on either side of them, and the equally terrifying army of Pharaoh right behind them. The author focuses on the hidden reflections of a young woman about the hard and dangerous journey she is on. Her ruminations say a lot about the anticipated joys of freedom from isolation and fear. Bear with the author as she reveals the secret thoughts of the woman in the story—who may be us. She writes:

> Her arms are laden with bracelets given to her by her former Egyptian mistress. She has coveted those bracelets for a long time and she knows that if her liberation is final they will be hers to keep. But somehow bracelets aren't as captivating when one is in the middle of a lightning storm with walls of water on either side, a hostile army in pursuit, and only a slippery ground to travel on. How is this woman to deal with her terror? She needs to keep on moving, step by step, to where the pillar of fire is leading her. She needs to deafen her ears, not to the howling wind or the whimpering of folks around her, but to the Pharaoh inside of her, her own fear.
>
> While in slavery, the woman unknowingly had created a Pharaoh inside her own skin. And the Pharaoh's voice is still inside her, louder than all the outside commotion. "You'll never make it," it says to her. "Where do you think you're going to stay when you get to the other side? A Holiday Inn? And even if there is a Holiday Inn there

on the other side, do you have a credit card? What makes you think that the God you are following is going to liberate you? Can you be sure that this leader Moses won't betray you? Do you think your God really wants you to become a fulfilled, happy person? Who do you think you are, anyway, you fool? Go back to where you belong—under my thumb."

It takes every ounce of courage and strength she possesses in order to stand up to the voice of the Pharaoh. She takes a deep breath and she says, "Shut up! I've had enough of it! I do matter! I do count! God values me! I can see God's light guiding me, even though it is ahead of me. There is ground beneath my feet, even though it's muddy and slippery. It is real and it holds me up and I can walk on it. And I will walk to the place where my God is leading me, where there is respect and meaning and real caring. I will not go back. I will let go of fear. I will not wear the bracelets of bondage. I will not be owned again."

And as she walks, she exhales terror and inhales strength and light, and she feels her back straighten and her head lift, and she notices that she has forgot the fear of the walls of water. She looks back and she sees Pharaoh's chariots sink their axles in the muck, and she looks ahead and sees the dim outline of the shore. Then she notices that the woman near her seems to have turned an ankle. She reaches out her hand to offer support. As she does so, her bracelets fall off into the mud. She doesn't even bother to pick them up. Instead, with her head held high, she looks ahead; clearly visible now is the light.

That's got to be one of life's greatest joys: to be liberated from fear and bondage, from the voice of the Pharaohs inside of us; that is to say, the voice of anyone in our lives that has put us down. Think for the moment of your friends or someone you know or even yourself who is *not* rejoicing because the voices won't let them. What voices? The Pharaoh voices that told them that they were stupid or fat or ugly. The voices that told them that they would never go anywhere in life. The voices that ignored them and lavished all their words of love on their brothers and sisters. The voices that trailed off from them, uninterested in them or what they had to say. The voices that ridiculed them. The voices that made fun of their defects: their ears are too big, their nose too long, their speech too stuttered, their brain too slow, their sports ability next to nothing, their popularity zero.

Think of the voices that might have mocked them when they prayed, "Do you think that God is really concerned about the likes of you?" The voices that told them they didn't count. The voices that told them they were ignorant and poor. The voices that should have spoken desperately needed words of encouragement and praise to them, but did not. The voices that never said to them, "I love you." The voices that told them of the impending separation and divorce.

Yes, so many voices that announced to them in many ways, "You'll never be free, never anything more than you are right now." These are the voices that keep them under Pharaoh's thumb. And maybe all those "thems" are us too. But imagine the joy of being liberated from such voices!

Is there anything we can do on Rejoice Sunday to make such people rejoice, to effect such liberation? Can we break open laughter in the universe? Can we drown out Pharaoh's voice? Of course we can, if for no other reason than we are here in the midst of a community that cares and we have a Lord who died for us, so much does he love us. We can remind people, and tell them over and over again with our voices, that they are good, indeed, made to the very image and likeness of God. We can introduce them to our community of faith that knows the voices of acceptance, sings the praises of a God who loves us and forgives us, and breaks a bread that tells us of the presence of the Risen Christ among us: the Light of the World, the light on the shore. We Christians can pick up the phone, send the card, remember the birthday, say "I love you." This day, this very day, we can offer people our presence, our faith, and our prayers—all unremarkable gestures that simply and unmistakably declare, "I see you and, what's more, Jesus sees you. And he likes what he sees."

And then, liberated by a new voice, they will begin to rejoice.

8

✛

Advertising for God

(John 3:14-21)

What may be of no interest to anybody in particular is that Yale University recently celebrated the bicentennial anniversary of the death of probably one of America's most creative geniuses, Ben Franklin. When he was sixteen years old, Ben Franklin published in a local paper of the time, the *New England Courant*, a series of essays now famously known, at least among scholars, as The Dogood Papers, so named after the character in these essays, a woman named Silence Dogood. And in those essays, Silence Dogood, who is a widow, announces her availability for marriage. And she sums up her desirable characteristics thus: "To be brief, I am courteous and affable, good-humored (unless I am first provoked), and handsome, and sometimes witty."

Ben Franklin died in 1790, leaving us with evidence of what in later times we would call personal ads. In fact, some scholar researched this whole area of personal ads and found that among English-speaking people, putting ads for dates, marriages, and things of that nature, in fact goes back even before Ben's time. For example, this researcher quotes a young man's ad in 1780 from North Britain who wrote, "I have very little brogue, and describe myself as tall in stature, finely shaped, and well-proportioned, have a delicate head of hair, a white hand, a large, strong back and broad shoulders," Well, in those agricultural days, these must have been very marketable attractions.

In 1903 *The Methodist Reporter* advertised for a pastor in the personal ads. The requirements? "Must have a small family, if any, and be able to furnish a horse, and come to church unassisted" (I presume that means he's not so decrepit that he can't walk to church). "Must not be afraid to work, have no hobbies, have a good, clear head, a warm, loving heart, and big feet." I'm not sure what the big feet refers to; maybe it's so he can't sneak up on people and catch them in their sins!

We have become somewhat more sophisticated and have advanced the personal ad to a high art. Probably the most widely read personal ads today are to be found in the back of the *New York Review of Books*. I culled a few of them. One says, "Here I am, unusual and good-looking, a thirty-seven-year-old woman sitting alone in my Manhattan apartment, wondering where all the aware, caring, generous, stable, and adventuresome gentlemen are." Another writes, "Handsome, New York City writer, fifty-four, seeks very attractive, bright, non-smoking woman, Dutch-treat, naturally. Telephone, etc." Another says, "Eastern university professor, sympathetic temperament, modest income, seeks wealthy widow for satisfied life." It *would* be a satisfying life if this professor of modest income found a wealthy widow. At least he's direct. And there's all the rest of the lonely hearts saying in effect, "I too am sitting in my apartment. Is there anybody out there who wants to share a life with me?"

Sometimes, to move the topic to another level, I think people would like to advertise, if they had the courage to, for God. And the reason why some might do that is because they struggle with the perennial question, "Where *is* God? Where is God in my life?" I think all of us would like to so advertise sometimes because at times God does seem quite absent. To all such seekers, however, today's gospel gives us its very famous and oft-quoted passage which, in effect, is a response to our ad for God. What does it say? It says, "God so loved the world that he sent his only-begotten Son so that those who believe in him may not perish, but have life everlasting."

A lot depends on the way you read that passage. The poignant reading emphasizes that "God *so* loved the world...." That's the Lover's cry and it's lovely. But our context today calls for this reading: "God so loved *the world*.." Yet, that God so loves this world is not particularly congenial to us because we have a heritage that says the opposite: "God must *hate* the world; it's such a dangerous, sinful, and corrupting place." And who can deny that everywhere you look there is war, hunger, greed, deceit, betrayal, abortion, infidelity, broken families, murder, accident, sickness, and all the rest of the familiar litany chanted by the anchor people of our nightly newscasts? No, our heritage says that, if you want to be saved, to be holy, then flee the world. Advertise for God, because God's not here, not on this planet.

And yet, here is our gospel this morning. Its radical Good News is that God loves the world, and not only does God love it but freely gave it his most precious gift, the Son. Surely God knew about sin and had already dealt with Cain and Abel, and Sodom and Gomorrah, and David and Bathsheba and all the rest of those wicked people that dot the Bible's pages. Yet, God insists that the world is lovable and that he loved it first, and is here waiting to be unmasked everywhere. The message is that it's a matter of uncovering and celebrating that presence, that love—yes, even in the midst of sin.

When I was a child in parochial school, we used to have to do a lot of memorizing, everything from the times tables to poetry. One of those poems I had to memorize with all the other children in the Catholic world—which I have now forgotten and had to look up again—is Joseph Mary Plunkett's poem, "I See His Blood." It may not be great poetry, but it translated John's gospel passage in its own way for us:

I see his blood upon the rose,
And in the stars, the glory of his eyes,
His body gleams amid the eternal snows,
His tears fall from the skies.

I see his face in every flower,
The thunder and the singing of the birds
Are but his voice, and carven by his power
Rocks are his written word.
All pathways by his feet are worn.
His strong heart stirs the ever-beating sea.
His crown of thorns is 'twined with every thorn.
His cross is every tree.

That's the poet's-eye view of our gospel. Its message is the same: God is not apart from the world but rather in it because God created it and loved it and sent Jesus into it. And in spite of all the evils that obscure the vision of God—which is a good definition of evil—God is here and we must learn to be alert to the Spirit and to hidden, everyday grace.

There is a famous theologian known perhaps not to the general public but surely to the members of his trade. His name is Edward Schillebeeckx and he has visited here and been to St. Mary's since he has relatives in town. I like this story he tells on himself. When he joined the Dominicans early on, they had to get up at two o'clock in the morning, like the monks, and then they would go to choir and chant the office. Young man that he was, just having entered the seminary, this lovely, monastic rising in the wee hours to sing God's praises quite captured his imagination and, thus apart from the noise and busyness of the world, he felt so close to God. So in his enthusiasm he wrote to his father, "How wonderful it feels to be praising God when all the world around me is asleep and I and my fellow seminarians are giving glory to God."

His father wrote back that he was glad that his young son appreciated his new monastic life, but he should remember that when he was an infant—he's one of thirteen children—his parents too were often up at 2 A.M. and, yes, they too were giving glory to God, although they weren't quite singing the psalms.

We tend to go with the Dominican, not with the father. "Get thee to the monastery and you'll find God," implied Edward. His father said, "No, it is in the everydayness of life that we uncover God, even if we do not realize it at the time." The spiritual and corporal works of mercy—those sole criteria from Jesus for being saved—are woven of grateful necessity into everyday life. God is there in the homework assisted, in the dishes done, in the hungry fed, in the comfort given, in the marketplace honored, in the business conducted. Indeed the monastery is important; no, even quite necessary, what we call reflective and retreat time, not as an escape or refuge from a godless world, but as a place to recover focus to seeing God there all the time, a reminder that "God so loved the world...."

If there is any lament that God has, it is that, after declaring that he so loved this world, that we wind up hating it, fascinated with the abuse and not the use of it for God's greater honor and glory. God has incarnated himself in the world, but we fail to recognize him. Somebody wrote a poem about that too, which is the opposite of the other poem. Let me share it with you. God is talking:

I am the great sun, but you don't see me.
I am your husband, but you turn away.
I am the captive, but you do not free me.
I am the captain you will not obey.

I am the truth, but you will not believe me.
I am the city, but you will not stay.
I am your wife, your child, but you will leave me.
I am the God to whom you will not pray.

I am your counsel, but you do not hear me.
I am your lover you will betray.
I am the victor, but you do not cheer me.
I am the holy dove whom you will slay.

I am your life, but if you will not name me,
Seal up your soul with tears, and never blame me.

I guess that's one good reason why we come to church: to recover our sense of vision, to celebrate the God we've bumped into all week without knowing it, to handle the Word and the Bread and to see this very congregation with the new realization that such common stuff indeed harbors the very presence of God. It's easy to become cynical, and it's natural to yearn for peace and quiet, for an end to the endless moral and physical pollution we experience every day, but it is Christian to praise God in spite of it all, to search for the Lord we know is hidden there, to sense ultimate goodness pulsating beneath the planet's movement, to praise beauty and truth which are also in great abundance on Earth, to be sensitive to love at every turn of life. Yes, we're here in this fellowship to learn to see God's face in every flower. Why? Because God so loved the world as to send the only-begotten Son into this very world so that those who believe—and discover—may not perish, but have life everlasting.

9

✝

The Failed Parent

(1 Samuel 2:12-17)

This is a two-part homily. The first part is dictated by the pressure of a war in Iraq called Desert Storm and the other part is, coincidentally, related to that country because the Scripture today talks about a man whose descendants had migrated a long time ago from Iraq.

Iraq was carved out of the old Ottoman Empire after World War I and, as so often happens, it was carved up without any particular regard to the various peoples there. So artificial boundaries were made that collected together the Chaldean, Kurdish, and Arabic peoples. Obviously, there would always be built-in tension and conflict.

But more to the point for us as a faith community is our general failure to realize that Iraq is the cradle of the three major faiths: Judaism, Christianity, and Islam. In a Scripture that all three faiths honor, the Book of Genesis, chapter two, verse ten, describes the Garden of Eden where it all began: "A river rises in the Garden of Eden toward the garden. Beyond there it divides and becomes four branches. The first is Pishon. The name of the second river is Gihon. The name of the third river is the Tigris, and the one that flows west of it is the Euphrates." And the land between the Tigris and Euphrates rivers, as some of you recall from your history, is the land then called Mesopotamia. The word is made up of *potmos*, which means river—as in hippopotamus, a "river horse"—and *meso*, a word that means between. And here was the location of our Garden of Eden: in the land between the two rivers, Mesopotamia. The Garden of Eden was in Iraq. That's worth thinking about.

Not only was the Garden of Eden in Iraq, according to the Bible, but also the two who started it all, Adam and Eve, lived there. According to our story, civilization and the human race began between the Tigris and Euphrates in Iraq. Furthermore, all three religions count one aged nomad as the ultimate source of faith. And that man, of course, is Abraham. Abraham was an Iraqi. It's good to remember that, too.

Nineveh, a town you might recall from the Book of Jonah, the reluctant prophet of whale-swallowing fame, is in northern Iraq. Babylon, that fabled city of the hanging gardens and mighty kings, is several miles south of Baghdad. It was these advanced and sophisticated inhabitants of Babylon who captured the Hebrews and sacked their city and leveled their Temple in 587 B.C. That was the beginning of the the legendary fifty-year Babylonian captivity, and much of the literature in the Old Testament from this period is filled with yearning for the homeland, with cries for liberation from exile. The book of Daniel was written about this era and some of the great prophets lived during this Babylonian-Iraqi exile, such as Jeremiah, Isaiah, and Ezekiel.

Christianity got to Iraq by way of St. Thomas the Apostle, it is said. It flourished there a good while until the seventh century when the Arab tribes from Saudi Arabia came in and swept Christianity away, bringing in Islam. In the thirteenth century, Genghis Khan invaded the country with his Mongolian hordes and took over Mesopotamia, as it was then called, until it became Persia. In the fourteenth century, the Tartars arrived and, as a result of their presence and that of all the others, there is only about five percent of Christianity left in Iraq now. The rest is divided among the various Muslim sects.

As we look at this war, in our faith community this morning, it is worth noting that Abraham was an Iraqi; that the three major faiths started with him; that the Garden of Eden, Adam and Eve, Cain and Abel, and all the rest—they were there. And so the war is more than some regional, distant conflict for us. It becomes both symbol and a commentary. The symbol is that you have Jews, Christians, and Arabs wiping out the memory of their common spiritual origin in the strafing and bombing and warring that is going on right now. They are blasting to smithereens their holy sites and erasing what binds them together spiritually. The commentary is that this is as good a definition of war as any: brothers and sisters killing each other and destroying what unites them, what makes them human, what makes them children of the one God they all believe in. Anyway, this little excursion is worth pondering.

But today's Scripture, as I said at the beginning, deals with a descendant of the man who came from Mesopotamia. His name is Eli and the little boy in the story is the future prophet Samuel. This little boy who lives in the Temple keeps hearing someone call his name at night and keeps running to old Eli, thinking it's he who's doing the calling, but it's not. Finally Eli figures it out, that it's God calling Samuel, and so he says to the little boy, "Look, the next time you hear someone calling you in the dark, say, 'Speak, Lord, for your servant is listening.'"

I don't want to deal with Samuel and I don't want to deal with his story, as touching as it is. I want to deal rather with Eli because you might remember that the Scripture said something else about Eli besides his being the high priest, namely, that he was a failed parent. Or at least he was a mightily disappointed parent. Both his sons, the Scripture makes clear, were scoundrels. The exact summary words concerning his sons are these: "They had no regard for the Lord." Does that sound familiar? Children have no regard for the Lord, for the old ways, for tradition. Children leave the faith, live in sin in various lifestyles that break their parents' hearts. Eli knew all about that. He grieved over such wayward sons.

This must have been extremely painful to Eli. After all, he was a man of position. He was a "man of the cloth," the high priest. People whispered behind his back that if he couldn't run his own sons how could he run a religious nation? Indeed, to have his children turn out so badly was a sad thing.

Eli's plight and Eli's voice can be found in its modern version, in a rather touching article in *Newsweek* entitled "Granny by Subpoena." It's by a woman named Sheila Evans. Let me share some of it. She writes:

My son called to tell me that the test results were in, and that I'm a grandmother. Cause for celebration? Well, not quite. My grandson is already four, lives with a woman I've never met, a woman my son met once. It was a party where they had too much to drink, one thing led to another and well, you get the picture. He fought the paternity suit all the way from blood test to DNA matching. Somebody fathered this dark-haired, dark-eyed child. My son is blond and blue-eyed. But my son sure hoped it wasn't him. He's twenty-nine and just starting a career, and the last thing he needed was a court order to send three hundred and fifty bucks a month to a stranger for the next fourteen years.

Part of me is sorry too, but I also think that somebody should support this youngster, preferably his parents. As a teacher, I've seen too many bewildered kids with absent parents, kids with no lifelines, no sense of the rules or the penalties when they're disregarded. Since there's no one at home to teach them the basics, they learn from a tough, unforgiving teacher, the real world. I hope this won't happen to my grandson, although having financial support is certainly no guarantee that it won't. So now I'm a grandmother. I thought it would never happen. My son is the youngest of three children, and both my daughters in their thirties are sure they don't want, and won't have, children. The only clock they hear ticking is the one in the board room. Kids are such an interruption in the career flow. So noisy and messy and inconvenient.

And then this "grandmother by subpoena" reminisces about when she had her children, about the great times she had with her own mother. They would meet and go to the park and go shopping and have lunch together. And she continues:

How silly I was, expecting to repeat the past. My daughters are too busy, embroiled in their own agenda of obligations and careers. No husbands. They can be as inconvenient as children, although not as permanent. Spending a day with my daughters would not only be an imposition, but a waste of time, since no one mends or irons any more.

And now my son tells me I'm a grandmother and I don't know what to do. My grandson should know his heritage. He should know that my people, hardy Kansas farm stock, live forever. My grandmother finally wore out at a hundred and five. I would like to walk in the park with this little guy, or feed the ducks with him. I could tell him many things. If we did get together, I wonder how he would react to a perfect stranger?

And this poignant lament is repeated countless times all over the country, isn't it? Grandparents raising grandchildren, children born out of wedlock, rerouted because of divorce, deposited because of career schedules, seeking court orders to visit one's grandchildren, being denied. Disappointed and failed parents. Yes, that theme is what our Scripture is about.

But the Scripture is about something else too. It has another and more hopeful note. It points out that, in spite of failure, God will not be without a voice and without a witness. And God will use a failed or disappointed parent to achieve this.

The boy Samuel, the great and future prophet of Israel, as we heard in the first reading, had his mind and spirit opened and sensitized by old Eli, the failed parent. Yes, this parent who could not open the minds and hearts of his own sons, taught another to listen to the voice of God. And that's the redeeming note of hope that today's reading offers. It says that for any of us—children or parents, spouses or friends, any of us who have experienced disappointed or failed relationships—we can still do much good because God offers us, always and at all times, a second career. It is as simple and powerful as that: We are offered a second career.

We can show the way to others and be there for others, even if we weren't successful with those closest to us. We can be teacher, guide, confidant, mentor, counselor, consoler, pray-er, and fellow pilgrim. And we will have even more impact and be more influential because our care and guidance and wisdom come from the hurts we have felt, the wounds we have known, the depths we have plumbed. In a word, all failed people can become wounded healers of others. We can be Eli to other Samuels not our own. We can teach others to hear when the Lord is calling, even if we missed it the first time around ourselves.

That's why I like the story of Eli. He must have been bitterly disappointed over his sons. He must have been sad that he, the religious leader, had two boys who no longer walked with the Lord, who took up another lifestyle. He must have prayed for them every day. He must have felt himself to be a useless and constant failure. But he had his moment and he seized it. This failed parent became mentor to one of the greatest prophets Israel ever had. He became a surrogate parent, a surrogate mentor, a surrogate saint for someone who needed him desperately, who was afraid of voices in the dark, and who welcomed his wisdom and comfort and became to him another and better child.

For any of us in this church right now who are Eli, heed the lesson, listen to the fullness of his story. Be comforted by what he did. Take heart in his second career and know that a second career—to be spiritual mentor, a witness to the truth, a guide, an advisor, a teacher of life to others—is open to every one of us. "Speak, Lord, for your servant is listening."

10

+

Returning

(Isaiah 55:6-9)

In the spirit of *glasnost*, I presume, an unusual film was permitted to be shown in Moscow about two years ago, entitled *Repentance*. It was such a popular film that it opened in seventeen Moscow theaters and the lines for tickets were even longer than the lines for the great Russian passion, the ballet. I read a review of that film in *The Christian Century* which described it as very searing, very poignant, very touching, and made all the more so by being set within the horrific Stalinist era.

In one episode of that surrealistic film, the people line up at the prison gate to get letters from relatives, and often on many of these letters are scribbled the words, "Left no forwarding address." The people look knowingly at each other. They all know what that means, and they weep. In another episode, the women are shown in a muddy timber yard, desperately picking up logs one by one and examining the ends of them. One woman finds her husband's name carved on one and weeping she caresses the log as if she were caressing her husband's face. The reviewer said he commented to a friend of his, "I suppose this is a kind of surrealistic statement." But the friend who was Russian replied that no, it was not. It was no statement, no dream. It was reality. "You see," he said, "it was common for people to search for the names on the end of logs because the prisoners who worked in the forests would carve their names and the last date as a sign that until at least that date, they were still alive."

And the film goes on to make of the women's insistent search for their husbands in a muddy timber yard a powerful parable of the Russian's search for God in a muddy society. In the midst of devastating and unrelenting horror, torture, and death they continued to look for God—and found God—even though the search was officially forbidden. And, finally, after that terrible era and with the fall of Communism, these same people and their children are flocking to the now open churches in the Soviet Union. No wonder the film is so popular for a people who, until recently, could not seek the Lord openly. How real and alive did they make today's first reading from Isaiah, "Seek the Lord while he may be found, call to him while he is near."

These people in a repressed society sought the Lord in their need for freedom and simple human dignity. Others in a free and open society like our own seek God because they discover that freedom and dignity without God are fragile things. I think of two people, two seekers, whose stories I would like to share with you. One is the author, novelist, and screenwriter, Dan Wakefield, who by his own admission was a former Christian, a fallen-away, leading the very dissolute life of celebrity high society and traveling the fast lanes of the New York-Hollywood jet setters. But one day he found himself, much to his surprise, seeking the Lord quite by accident. It seems that he happened to be in Boston and went to King's Chapel for no other reason than it was Christmas and on Christmas this is what people do: go to church. So he stumbled into church because he had nothing better to do and, besides, he wrote, all the bars were closed. But, in spite of himself, in the quiet of that chapel, seeing the Christ Child there, that gentle God-in-the-flesh, he was caught by old memories and a new emptiness in his life. Something resonated in his soul.

And it wasn't long before he returned, returned to his roots, to Christ. And he wrote a very beautiful book about that return called *Returning* which has been compared to St. Augustine's *Confessions*. He sought and he found. The crib and its memories had caught him.

The other story I would share comes from a surprising source, the sophisticated *New England Monthly*. The writer is a young woman, twenty-eight years old, named Catherine Whitemore. And in contrast to a St. Augustine and in contrast to a Dan Wakefield, she did not suddenly stumble once again onto Christ and church. No, she took the typical yuppie, tryout consumerist view of her return to religion and treated her search, in our estimation, rather lightly. She had a kind of "pick and choose" quality to her return to church.

She grew up Episcopal and her religious memories, good memories, she writes, go back to coloring books in Bible school and the crucifix over her bed. And that was about it. In college she continued her search for God somewhat, but admits, "I rarely went to church, and indeed, I scoffed at the organized religion of my upbringing." But by and by she got interested in church once again and found herself, like Dan Wakefield, in the Boston-Cambridge area and on the day she thought she might like to try out church again, she simply turned to the yellow pages! She found forty-eight listings of the Episcopal church. So she said she chose one, the Harvard Cambridge Church, but she found it to be more social and political than theological, adding that "I was almost embarrassed to admit that."

She tried another church famous for its choir and liturgy. It was a big architectural landmark and she found a certain comfort and anonymity here. But on the other hand, she said, she felt she was being a part of an audience, not personally engaged. And so she went to still another church where the minister was very good, but he moved and so she moved too. This approach may strike us as a "pick and choose" kind of religion, but nevertheless she was searching for the Lord and would not be put off. Where did she wind up? She wound up with a simple church that preached and lived the cross of Jesus Christ. It wasn't the music, the liturgy, or the minister, but it was the Lord and the Crucified Lord at that.

She quotes the great writer Martin Buber that "religion is essentially the act of holding fast to God," and then she adds herself, "and church-going is merely one way to tighten the grip." But, most of all, she testifies, "It's difficult to explain exactly why I go, but I suppose the reason is this: in a soft life it is good to hear hard words." Her words rang a bell and I went back to T.S. Eliot and found these lines in his poem, *The Rock*, where the chorus says:

Why should men love the church?
Why should they love her laws?
She tells them of life and death
and all they would forget.
She is tender where they would be hard
and hard where they would like to be soft,
She tells them of evil and sin
and other unpleasant facts.

It's interesting, the paths of these two seekers, Dan Wakefield and Catherine Whitemore. One is captured by the crib and the other by the cross, and both by the memories they stirred up. I suppose that's all I want to do: share their stories and give hope to those whose family or friends have left the church. But we should not gloss over the underlying dynamic; namely, that the basic testimony of both people is that their return was precisely that: a *return*. That is to say, someone had already in their young years laid a foundation. There were pictures and prayers and Bible school and family church-going and all the rest. Later on, it is true, they left all that, but *it did not leave them*. Grace was but dormant, merely waiting to be resurrected by the crib or the cross of another time. It was there, put there by someone significant.

Their stories, therefore, remind us of the importance of laying good foundations, of the rightness of your being here, the praise you are giving God, the worship together, the example and witness—in short, the memories you are creating for this community, this parish, this family. Never underestimate the power of memories. Whether you teach others the gentleness and nearness of the crib or the demands and cost of the cross, do it early, do it often, do it faithfully, do it with your own lives. Never forget Isaiah's message, "Seek the Lord while he may be found, and call to him while he is near." If you don't forget, someone, someday, will remember.

11

✛

Baptism: The Crisis of Identity

(Mark 1:7-11)

Today is the feast of the baptism of Jesus. Christians who are perplexed over why Jesus was baptized, since he had no original sin to be rid of, might be relieved to know they're in good company. That's because even the people of Jesus' own time wondered about it and were embarrassed over the whole episode. And they would have gotten rid of the whole incident, except that it was so strong in the tradition that they couldn't. It really happened: Jesus was baptized. But their embarrassment was of a different order, namely, Jesus the greater was baptized by John the lesser and it should have been the other way around. So Matthew has John protest, "I need to be baptized by you and do you come to me?" And Jesus answers that it's the way to "fulfill all righteousness." John omits the actual baptism and Luke sidesteps the issue by having John the Baptist in prison before Jesus' baptism and simply states in the passive voice that Jesus was baptized, and lets it go at that.

But, beyond the controversies, baptism had a deeper meaning. It meant conversion. Not necessarily a conversion from sin, but rather a conversion, a "turning toward" a particular way of life. In other words, baptism was also considered to be a mandate, an inauguration to a mission. It was a public event for all to see that put one on the spot, something like getting married, declaring one's love and commitment publicly to this very special person so that all the world knows the two are one. Or something like declaring one's candidacy, not for political public office, but for the public office of Christian, a follower of Jesus. So for Jesus himself, his baptism was not a cleansing from sin, but something in its deeper sense: a public declaration of his mission. From that point on he would be defined as God's Son, God's envoy, God's prophet, God's lover. "I come to do will of him who sent me" was his declared motto at his baptism.

Being defined is something we know about in our modern world. And it is incredibly important. We call it, honed as we are by a pervasive media, image-making. Corporations are defined by their logos. Michael Jordan is defined by his celebrity status as a great basketball player. Madonna is defined by her videos and the fifty-nine million dollars we heaped on her last year. Donald Trump is defined by his wealth and his women. People have always been defined by their logos or names or nicknames that history bequeathed to them. That's one level. But more serious definitions that impinge on the public welfare are surrounded by elaborate public ceremonies such as the swearing in of the president. Others get their definition from history, which looks back to acknowledge their contributions. Alexander, for example, earned the addition "the Great" because he was such an extraordinary military leader. Then you have Ivan the Terrible, William the Conqueror, Lorenzo the Magnificent, Richard the Lion-Hearted, John the Baptizer, and, yes, even Hagar the Horrible. And you have Jesus who is called the Christ, a title that means "anointed one," a title he received at the public ceremony of his image–making, his office-taking, his baptism. "This is my beloved Son," said the voice from heaven. "My favor rests on him." The ceremony and the mission were ratified.

And so, seeing Jesus' baptism that way throws a lot of light on our own baptism. Our baptism defines us publicly in relationship to God and consequently to one another, who pray openly, *Our* Father. It defines us as a child of God, as being related to God and God's work. The baptism we have undergone enrolls us in the public office of Christian. And it is good to remember that what we do unconsciously when we enter church, dipping our hand in the holy water font—a miniature baptismal font—is meant to renew our sense of baptism, a reminder that we belong to God, not privately as in some clandestine relationship, but publicly, committedly, openly. We have a mission to make this world holy by our holy lives. We are God's beloved son, beloved daughter in a most profound sense. That becomes our foundational definition and identity.

The trouble is that because of the culture and mass media atmosphere we are in, who we are and what we are as God's children becomes easily challenged and even obscured. We are bombarded with a million other images that challenge us, "Why don't you be like this?" or "You should be like that. This is the current 'look,' the current 'in' images, the current persona." "You have an inadequate if not poor image" is the motto of all advertising. "We will make you over." For a price, of course. That is why the reports all tell us that girls in particular are subject to depression more easily than boys, especially as they enter teenage. The media imagery of the female, an impossibly celluloid, manipulated image, is nigh impossible to achieve, and depression sets in when it isn't. We are consistently told to be other than what we are, because what we are is inadequate. Our main mission, they tell us, is not to be holy and make the world holy; our main mission is to be beautiful and to feel good about ourselves. We are nothing if we are *merely* ourselves, the "merely" subverting altogether any sense of being made in God's image, touched by the Spirit, affirmed in our identity and dignity at baptism, and loved madly by God.

Jules Pfeiffer is a humorist who writes plays and does clever, satirical cartoons. He has one series of panels that goes like this. It's a boy named Danny talking. "Ever since I was a little kid I didn't want to be me. I wanted to be like Billy Whittleton, and Billy didn't even like me. I walked like he walked; I talked like he talked. I signed up for the same high school he signed up for, which was when Billy Whittleton changed. He began to hang around with Herbie Vanderman. He walked like Herbie Vanderman; he talked like Herbie Vanderman. And then it dawned on me that Herbie Vanderman walked and talked like Joey Hamerlin. And Joey Hamerlin walked and talked like Corky Fabinson. So here I am, walking and talking like Billy Whittleton's imitation of Herbie Vanderman's version of Joey Hamerlin trying to walk and talk like Corky Fabinson. And who do you think Corky Fabinson is always walking and talking like? Of all people, dopey Kenny Wellington—that little pest who walks and talks like me!"

Archbishop Tutu, the black Anglican archbishop in South Africa, says he always preaches one message to his people there. His message is simple and he repeats it over and over again. It is that "God loves you." "I tell them that," he says, "because the entire culture tells them that they are unlovable, and I have to give them the message of who they really are, because God loves them."

The other day I was looking over the biography of George Washington Carver, the great black scientist who did a lot with the lowly peanut, both medically and commercially. He made it a great industry through his scientific endeavors. Back in the early 1900s when prejudice was even more rampant than today, he always used to tell the black community not to let themselves be defined by those who are prejudiced against them. He was a religious man and he believed mightily in his baptism that defined him first as a child of God. And he demonstrated it.

He was brought to Washington, D.C., to the Ways and Means Committee in January 1921 to explain his work on the peanut. He expected such a high-level committee to handle the business at hand with him and those who had come with him with dignity and proper decorum. He was shocked when speakers who got up ahead of him to make their presentations were treated in a very demeaning manner and harassed. As a black man, he was last on the list and so, after three days, he finally walked up the aisle to speak. And on the way up he heard one of the committee members say—and quite loudly for all to hear—"I suppose you have plenty of peanuts and watermelon to keep you happy!" He ignored the remark as an ignorant jibe, although it stung him. He was further hurt on seeing another committee member sitting there with his hat on and his feet on the table. When the chairman of the Ways and Means Committee told the member to take off his hat, he said out loud, "Down where I come from we don't accept any nigger's testimony, and I don't see what this fellow can say that has any bearing on this committee."

At this point George Washington Carver was ready to turn around and go back home, but he said, as he wrote in his autobiography, "Whatever they said of me, I knew that I was a child of God, and so I said to myself inwardly, 'Almighty God, let me carry out your will.'" He got to the podium and was told that he had twenty minutes to speak. Carver opened up his display case and began to explain his project. Well, so engaging was his discussion that those twenty minutes went all too quickly and the chairman rose and asked for an extension so he could continue his presentation, which he did for an hour and three-quarters. They voted him four more extensions so he spoke for several hours. At the end of his talk they all stood up and gave him a long round of applause. And all because he knew who he was and because he refused to be defined by the labels of his culture.

"Whatever they said of me, I knew I was a child of God." That's what baptism is all about, Jesus' and our own. Positively, baptism is a basic, irreversible identity and dignity as God's child with all the commitment to mission that that implies; negatively, it resists being defined by the culture otherwise, no matter how nasty or seductive that culture. And—no doubt about it—at times, like Jesus, the baptismal identity and the culture's identity will clash and we will have a crisis. Will we hold fast to what we are under God, or jettison that for the more appealing identity of power? "Fall down and adore me and all these things will be yours" is a constant temptation.

But baptism says we should not any longer be defined by others. Blacks should not be defined by whites, and vice versa. Men and women should not be defined by each other. The oppressed should not be defined by their oppressors. The culture should not define us out of our basic identity. St. Paul put it rightly and directly: "For in Christ Jesus you are all children of God. For as many of you *as were baptized* there is neither Jew nor Greek, there is neither slave nor free, there is neither male nor female, for you are all one in Jesus Christ."

So we end where we began. Why does the church make a fuss over the baptism of Jesus? Why was he baptized anyway? He was baptized as a sign of public commitment and public definition of who he was. "You are my beloved Son." Your baptism and mine are the same. We have been defined forever as God's children, and no one should be allowed to take that identity from us, or deface it, or make us ashamed of it. And we have been given a mission at baptism: to do the works of Christ, to continue his mission. We can be no more than that; we are never any less.

Baptism makes us "beloved children" forever.

12

+

The Scribe

(Mark 12:28-34)

There is a fruitful and obvious theme in today's gospel that I'm going to resist dealing with, namely, Jesus' famous answer of the dual commandments of love of God and love of neighbor, and how he intertwined them. The reason for that is that, before we ever get to the answer of Jesus there is something else that intrigues me, or, I should say, *someone* else. It's the man who asked the question in the first place, the scribe who provoked the answer, the scribe who in those days was roughly equivalent to a lawyer. But, first, a significant context. This incident comes right after some very unpleasant and very hostile encounters Jesus had with the Pharisees and Sadducees—and they didn't come off too well. These opposing religious-political parties hated each other and only teamed up to use Jesus to score off of each other, and also make him out to be unfaithful to the traditions of the nation.

And so, when we get to the scribe in our gospel story today, what we have is a lawyer who has been hired by the bruised opposition to embarrass the defendant. As front man for the still tender Pharisees and the Sadduccees, the scribe poses a favorite traditional and endlessly debated question to Jesus, one that for centuries the rabbis and the lawyers have puzzled over and argued about. Where did this amazing new teacher stand on the age-old debate: of the 613 laws that Moses had given to the people of Israel, which one was the greatest? Of course, no matter which one Jesus picked, he was bound to offend some party who thought that one of the other 612 was most important. It was a no-win situation. So the scribe's question, "What is the greatest commandment?" is a well-known trap; and it is obvious that the scribe is coming from deceit and not sincerity, with the Pharisees and the Sadducees who put him up to it silently standing there and delighting in the dilemma.

But, as they say, something happened on the way. Jesus gives the scribe such a stunning answer that it catches him in the middle of his conscience and fundamental decency, which have been dormant for many years. And you can almost sense it. After Jesus' reply, there is a long period of silence as the scribe stands there, struggling between his loyalty to his party bosses, not to mention his own status, and this insight and rightness of the truth that he had just heard from the teacher who looked at him, not with triumph, but with love. He finally reaches his moment of truth. He turns his back on the establishment and he says slowly to Jesus, "You are right in saying that the love of God and the love of neighbor are more important than all the burnt offerings and sacrifices one could make." And then in turn the scribe heard what is indeed a very great thing to be told, "You are not far from the reign of God."

And that's all we hear of the scribe. We are not told what happened to him afterwards, whether he lost his job or lost his friends or ran into the unaccountable reality of his clients suddenly fading away. Or perhaps, was there an incident like Atticus's in To Kill a Mockingbird where people spat in his face and called him traitor? We don't know what happened to him. But whatever, the gospel clearly means to pass on to us a story of conversion. The scribe moves from deceit to sincerity. The scribe lets his basic decency, so long overshadowed by ambition and self-service, become active once more. His encounter with Jesus, the gospel implies, brought him back to the center of things and restored his integrity. All the debates and tricky questions he was so good at simply became secondary to the realities of the truth he had just heard.

I don't know if you are, but I'm fascinated by this scribe. I find that he is a type. He's like some of those people you read about in novels or see in the movies where, say, the female agent is hired to seduce a counteragent and kill him, and she winds up falling in love with him. That sort of thing. He reminds me in modern times of John Dean of the Watergate disgrace, suddenly recognizing his "blind ambition" (the name of his book) and moving from intrigue to confession. Or Charles Colson, another Watergate scoundrel, moving from deceit to true and deep sincerity when he met Jesus Christ after the disgrace was over. He reminds me of the recently deceased Malcolm Muggeridge. Some of you may know his name. The editor of the famed British magazine, *Punch*, he was a very famous, very witty man, a fantastic writer, and darling of the upper crust. And he had a scribe experience. He set out to deceive and to mock Jesus but like the scribe, he was caught by him. Toward the end of his long life, he wrote these words:

I may, I suppose, regard myself, or pass for being, a relatively successful man. People occasionally stare at me in the street. That's fame. I can fairly earn enough money to qualify for admission to high society. That's success. Furnished with money and a little fame, even the elderly, if they care to, may partake of trendy diversions. That's pleasure. It might happen once in a while that something I wrote or said was sufficiently heeded for me to persuade myself that it represented a serious impact on our time. That's fulfillment. And yet I say to you, and I beg you to believe me, multiply these tiny triumphs by a million, add them all together, and they are nothing, less than nothing, measured against one draft of the living water that Jesus Christ offers to the spiritually thirsty, irrespective of who and what they are.

There's a scribe not far from the reign of God.

But our gospel scribe, as I see him, is more than John Dean or Charles Colson or Malcolm Muggeridge. The scribe is a type, often found in or out of the church. He's the one, or she's the one, with the trenchant criticisms and the angry denunciations of churchy matters. They can wax righteously and eloquently, often with insight and truth, about certain deficiencies of the church and organized religion: the scoundrels who misuse money, scandalous priests, birth control, divorce, premarital sex, abortion. As if these things were the heart of the matter and all that mattered. They can crusade tirelessly and debate endlessly about principles, can talk and write marvelously. They spar and they maneuver. They're clever and resourceful. Their critiques are right on target. They can set a hundred traps. But they haven't come to terms with the basics and they even use their brilliance to keep the basics at bay. And those basics come from Jesus who, cutting through it all, asks them how they treat their families, how they hug their children, how they tend their neighbor, how they comfort the sorrowing, how they feed the hungry, how they visit the sick. The thing is they never seem to get around to the practical basics of the love of God and the love of neighbor. They are like the scribe who is wrapped up in the issues and never quite gets around to people.

In one way or other, on another level from the constant critics, we are all somewhat into being scribes. We are dedicated to a thousand good causes: careers, projects, programs, hobbies, agendas, schedules, and what have you. We know the ins and outs of our fields. We are a busy people. But the two great commandments: do they operate? A man was telling me about his wife who is very sick with a poor heart and in need of constant care and hospitalization. They have a nephew to whom they were very good when he was growing up. They helped him through school and gave him and his friends hospitality more times than they can remember. He is now a famous cardiologist in this country and goes all over the world giving lectures and consultations. He knows his aunt is sick. Yet not once in the last two years has he either stopped by or called to see how she is. Like the scribe, he's into the big issues. After all, he is brilliant and he knows many things. What he doesn't know is the greatest of all: how two commandments are one. Is he us?

I think the Christian community saved this story because it knew there would be scribes in every age of the church. But it also knew that someday most people would come up against a truth so simple, so profound, so stated with love that it would be for them their moment of truth. The gospel offers us that truth. It even offers us a model of conversion in the story of the scribe, a story that tells us that if we have the courage to turn our backs on our vested interests we become heirs to the promise: "You are not far from the reign of God."

13

+

Slouching Toward Bethlehem

(Matthew 2:1-12)

Whatever terrors the Arabian desert held for our soldiers during the Gulf War of 1991, it did hold out one reward. In that place where the horizon is absolutely endless, the sky incredibly wide and all-embracing, and where artificial lights of filament and neon are absent, the stars are a sight to see. They are brilliant, bright, multitudinous, magnificent, and seemingly almost within touch. Any soldier in the desert could appreciate why the ancient travelers over that ocean of sand navigated their caravans by these brilliant stars and learned to read the sky as well as we can read a Rand-McNally map.

At this time of the year, of course, we are interested in a certain group of travelers in that desert, travelers conjured up by Matthew to provide all generations with an ancient insight to the Child who was about to be born, that this Child was indeed for all ages, for all peoples, for all places, for all times. From north to south, from east to west, God is Emmanuel, "with us."

In any case, who would these prophetic figures of high imagination be for Matthew? What would be their context, their origin, and what would subsequent ages make of them?

The context is an old one. One of the great religions of the time was the Persian one, Zoroastrianism. There are probably only about a hundred twenty thousand followers today of the Persian prophet, Zoroaster, who lived about six hundred years before Christ. Most of them are now in India because there was a Muslim uprising and they fled to India; most of them are in Bombay. They are among the most intelligent and cultured people on Earth. They are exceedingly bright, sophisticated, and very generous. In fact, they are the highest philanthropic group on record; and so if the ideal is that you live what you say and preach, these Zoroastrians come off very well. However, if you're thinking of joining them, you can't because you can only come into this religion by birth, not by conversion. That's why their numbers are small; and, like most sophisticated and well-off people everywhere, they have few children. The well-known conductor, Zubin Mehta, is a Zoroastrian.

The reason I mention the Zoroaster religion is because Matthew says in his gospel that when Jesus was born, Wise Men came from the East to Jerusalem asking, "Where is he who has been born the King of the Jews? We have seen his star in the East." Now, although many translations are given—Magi, magicians, astrologers—it is very likely that these so-called wise men were priests of the Zoroaster religion. And one of the clues to this guess is their constant reference to the star, because it is their belief that every good person has a guiding light in the heavens that appears as a star; and the greater the person born, the brighter the star in the heavens. Now that would figure: as Zoroastrian priests, they saw this bright star and knew that there was a great person who had been born somewhere. As a matter of fact, the Zoroastrians worship the god of light, Ahura Mazda, which is one of the early names for the electric light, and it's also the name of a company that produces electric bulbs today. The reference is to the Zoroastrian god of light.

And so the most intelligent guess about Matthew's symbol of a universal salvation, which included such gentiles as the

Magi, is that as Zoroastrian priests they worshipped the god of light and believed that every great person had a bright star. No wonder they trekked across the desert in search of the one whose bright star was extraordinary.

Their number? That has varied with imagination. Sometimes the number was given as twelve, but often the number was given as six. The six got entrenched because in Milan, Italy, supposedly, three relics of the Magi were honored. But in 1164 there was an uprising and the relics were moved to Cologne, Germany. But in time people didn't know that bit of history and so they figured there were three relics in Italy and three in Germany and that equals six Magi. Finally, imagination worked backwards and figured that since there were three gifts mentioned—gold, frankincense, and myrrh—this suggested Three Givers. Thus our Zoroastrian priests have come down to us as the Three Wise Men.

But the impulse of storytelling could never let Matthew's tale rest there, and in fact it took a clue from Matthew himself by reaching back to the Old Testament. There it found a psalm, the very responsorial psalm we used today, Psalm 72, whose refrain says, "The Kings of Arabia will come bearing gifts." This psalm was applied to the Magi and so the unnumbered priests of Zoroaster were turned into Three Kings. "We Three Kings of Orient Are" is our musical testimony to this development.

How about their names? In Matthew's version there are no names. Some would speculate that this was done on purpose and was consistent with Matthew's story. Since mad King Herod was running all over killing anybody connected with the Christ Child, Matthew didn't want to use the names of the Magi since they and their descendants would thereby be in peril of their lives. But once more imagination could not abide that lack for long and thus long after wicked Herod died, names were found. In fact, the names we have today were first found in those fabulous sixth-century mosaics in Ravenna, Italy: Balthazar, Melchior, and Gaspar.

Even the gifts took on symbolism. Gold equals the virtue of

these travelers. Frankincense, which is like incense going up to heaven, says they were a people of prayer, daily lifting their prayers to God. And myrrh, which is bitter and a kind of mineral, means they were willing to take on the bitterness and sacrifice necessary in their pursuit of the Holy One of Light.

Other stories and legends clustered around these very exotic people. One legend says that when they were over a hundred years old, they met again in 54 A.D. in Armenia to attend Midnight Mass, and then died shortly after. Another says they went to India where they were consecrated bishops by Thomas the Apostle and they died in their dioceses. Another legend, which I like, says that they were of three different ages. Gaspar was a very young man. Balthazar was in his middle age, and Melchior was an old man. When they arrived at Bethlehem, the three of them betook themselves into the cave of the Savior's birth and they went in one at a time. When Melchior, the old man, went into the cave, there was no one there but a very old man his own age with whom he was quickly at home. And they spoke together of memory and of gratitude. The middle-aged Balthazar encountered a middle-aged teacher when he went into the cave and they talked passionately of leadership and responsibility. And when young Gaspar entered, he met a young prophet, and they spoke words of reform and promise. And then when they had all gone outside after going in one by one, the three of them took their gifts and went in together. And when they went in together there was nobody there but a twelve-day-old infant. And later on they understood. The Savior speaks to every stage of life. The old hear the call to integrity and wisdom. The middle-aged hear the call to generativity and responsibility. And the young hear the call to identity and intimacy.

Truly, the Three Wise Men have caught our imagination, and noticeably more so than the other group in Matthew's Christmas story. And there is, I think, a powerful reason for that. That other group is the shepherds. Have you noticed that the shepherds have never really caught our imaginations and that we have few stories about them? The reason is that, in the gospels, the shepherds are told everything. They are encountered by a very talkative angel. And this angel tells them every detail: where the Child is to be found, who's there, how to get there. When the shepherds arrive at the cave, the angel appears again to verify the place, and when the shepherds return they're guided by a whole heavenly choir of angels singing to them along the way. So these shepherds have no doubts, no questions, no problems, no persecutors, no mystery. They didn't have to seek information. It was handed to them. They had it made.

That's not our experience. The easy-come, easy-go shepherds are not for us. Our experience is more likely the struggling Magi. We, like them, are searchers. We have difficulty with the large questions of life. We are harassed by our modern Herods who seek to destroy our children with consumerism, materialism, greed. We wonder about family life, AIDS, crime in the streets, illness, cancer, war, recession, death. Yes, we too would like heavenly messengers and heavenly assurances such as the shepherds got, but the fact is we experience neither. No, no doubt about it, it's the Magi, the struggling band crossing a hot desert with only a vision and hope to guide them, that resonates with us. They're our kind of people and we'll never tire of telling stories about them.

So, we'll stick with them because the bottom line is that they are searchers and so are we. But they are searchers who have taught us something. They searched together and have left us the clear message that we must always do the same. We can't search, we can't travel, and we can't find alone. We need one another and that's why we're here this morning. This is why we "come to church." Alone, we tend to become idiosyncratic, distorted, and lost. We need the collective wisdom of the community. We need the collective support and prayers of our fellow pilgrims. There's more than the sum total of people here when all of us chorus together, "Lord, have mercy on us!" and, like the Magi, search the ancient Scriptures together. We are a caravan. We are a church. We listen together. We pray together. We cry out together. We are strengthened and comforted by each other. There's no other way to travel.

The Magi didn't have all the answers. Neither do we. They had a wicked King after them. In many ways so do we. But on their life travels what they did have was fellowship and the light of Christ to guide them. And so do we. But the best part of the wondrous Magi story comes at the end: they left us a promise. For at last they found what they were looking for. And so will we.

14

✛

The Radical Gospel

(Matthew 25:31-46)

The Christian writer, C.S. Lewis, who had the misfortune to die the same day President John F. Kennedy was assassinated, made this comment.

> When we get to heaven, there will be three surprises: First, we will be surprised by the people that we find there, many of whom we surely had not expected to see. The second surprise is that we will be surprised by the people who are absent—the ones we did expect to see but who are not there. The third surprise, of course, will be that we're there.

Just what the gospel says: the saved and the unsaved, the sheep and the goats will be separated by the fundamental criterion of the spiritual and corporal works of mercy and not by status, income, or social position. And what a surprise that will be to many. Another great Christian writer, Frederick Buechner, expresses the same thought: "Many an atheist is a believer without knowing it. Just as many a believer is an atheist without knowing it. You can sincerely believe there is no God and live as though there is one. You can sincerely believe there is a God and live as though there is not." The gospel says that, to the surprise of many, it will all come out in the end.

Let's translate, then, the challenge implicit in the gospel into today's headlines. On one day, it so happened, three articles appeared on the very same front page of the *New York Times.* One article began:

> Financial institutions are falling and bread lines are lengthening. But as usual there's no recession among the purveyors of diversion. Jack Nicholson got ten million dollars for joking around in *Batman.* Buster Douglas got twenty-four million for the seven minutes it took him to lose the heavyweight crown. And Bill Cosby who has an income of a hundred million dollars a year could double the gross national product of many a small country simply by moving there.

The article also noted that Michael Jackson who gets eighteen million dollars an album is now negotiating upwards for twenty-five million dollars per record. And all indications are that he will get it. He will be the highest paid entertainer who ever lived.

The second article had this headline: "A crowd of 162 in millionaire baseball lineup." It points out that more than one-fifth of the major league players are millionaires and more. Twenty-two percent of big leaguers were paid at least a million dollars this year. Last year the Mets alone, for example, led with nine one-million-dollar players. At the end of 1991 the Mets' twenty-nine-year-old Bobby Bonilla was guaranteed twenty-nine million dollars for five years to play baseball. So those nine people out there on the field means that you and I are paying to watch millionaires play ball.

The third article's headline noted, "Where all that gas goes: the drivers' thirst for power." It points out that one reason that Americans, who make up only four percent of the world population, consume forty percent of its gasoline, is that they like the more powerful, less fuel-efficient engines in cars. One car dealer is quoted as saying, "Drivers may not do the calculations that they need to do." Car dealers say that the economy seems to be hardly a consideration for most buyers.

So there we have it. On one typical front page of a newspaper we have a pop singer who gets twenty-five million dollars a record, another entertainer who makes over one hundred million dollars a year, baseball players who are millionaires and four percent of Americans consuming forty percent of the world's gasoline. But in almost an unconscious parallel with today's gospel, the inside pages of that same newspaper have an account of the International Conference on the state of children in the world. Every year, the conference points out, fourteen million children die unnecessarily from hunger and malnutrition, and the lack of ordinary, common medical care. They die, but all of those fourteen million deaths are easily preventable. Even Oprah Winfrey remarked about this on her TV show. She pointed out that it takes only nineteen cents a week, less than ten dollars a year, to feed a child. Others have noted that if as little as ten percent of the military budget went into these fourteen million children's feeding, they would live.

Today, as I speak to you, before midnight strikes, statistically thousands of children will die from measles, tetanus, and diphtheria because they have not been immunized with a vaccine that costs a dollar. Additional thousands of children will die today of respiratory infection because they can't afford a dollar's worth of antibiotics. And still more thousands of children will die today from diarrhea and dehydration because their parents don't know how to treat them with a simple remedy of sugar, salt, and water costing only a few cents. And in our own country, twenty percent of America's children live below the poverty line.

You take these contrasts and suddenly you appreciate how radical today's gospel is. It's a gospel that says that a culture that supports millionaire ballplayers and other entertainers but cannot come up with a dollar's worth of sugar and salt is in for a surprise. The goat population will have some notables among it.

But that's the plight of the goats. The gospel does mention sheep, those who saw life differently and reacted differently and perhaps were unsurprised to find themselves on the right hand of the Lord. I'd like to say something about those sheep. Or, in this case, a certain sheep who is an American missionary priest in Korea. He wrote an article in *Maryknoll* magazine entitled, "Why I Became a Foreign Missionary." He writes very simply, without bragging, and presents us with five episodes and ends each episode with the refrain, "This is why I became a missionary priest."

First episode. There is a massive street protest. The priest joins in because the people are protesting against many injustices in this semi-totalitarian country. Accompanying photos show three Franciscan friars in their familiar brown habits, all of them Korean, sitting in the front of the crowds during the protest. Right into the front line the soldiers fire tear gas. The crowd has to scatter. He writes, "Suddenly someone is seeking shelter behind a shattered shop and reaches out to hand me a moist towel and says, 'Thank you, Father.' It is for that I became a missionary priest."

Second episode. "One Sunday morning an old man lies in a drunken stupor along the curb of a busy street. People pass him by. Cars barely miss him. I, too, am in a hurry, on my way to offer Mass at a nearby parish, when a disturbing parable comes to mind. I stop and offer him a hand. Two men suddenly appear and assist and carry him off to safe quarters."

Third episode. "A Catholic woman has been fired from a factory for suggesting that workers have a right to go to the bathroom periodically. She stands alone in protest outside the factory gate. A local priest tells the Legion of Mary about her. A group of grandmothers, armed with rosaries, take their place beside the woman at the gate. Before long she gets her job back."

Fourth episode. Late one night there's a knock at the gate. A young woman stands with her son in the dark. Both are crying. Her husband is in a drunken rage. Fearing for her safety and that of her son, she comes to us. She has nowhere else to go and no one else to turn to.

Final episode. This is his reflection on a Sunday Mass. The church where it is celebrated is a huge, open shed. It is crowded. For this missionary it is a familiar scene, but as he says, "You can be surprised by God. As people come forward to receive communion, I find myself entranced by the many faces: old and wizened, young and vibrant, pained and searching. Each is the image of God. Their faces reflect faith that it is Jesus they are receiving. Each face seems to say, 'With you I am one of God's people, the Body of Christ.'" And this priest concludes his recollection of each episode with the words, "It is for this I became a missionary priest."

The front page stories of the luxurious excesses of the few and the inside pages of the needs of the many are the dividing line between the sheep and the goats. The lifestyles of the rich and famous and the compassion and service of an American friar in Korea are the dividing line between the sheep and the goats. That's how this gospel translates today.

What about us? We are certainly not a cruel or indifferent people. We are truly generous, caring, and sensitive. But—we are also culturally conditioned to allow a performer to make twenty-five million dollars while fourteen million children die from malnutrition. We are culturally conditioned by a massive advertising system that insulates us from the needs of others. "Alive with pleasure" and "You've come a long way, baby" are not slogans that hang in the emphysema or cancer wards. Our Christmas catalogues do not carry pictures of shrunken, swollen Ethiopian babies. And that's why the gospel is so radical and uncomfortable. It dares to lift up society's hem, like Scrooge's ghost of the future, to reveal the twin orphans of ignorance and poverty.

Well, obviously, the gospel, which is a gospel of judgment, calls for some kind of a response. And there is one, one given context by an experience I had years ago when I visited Germany and its Dachau prison. That prison, now a museum to horror and spirit, is filled with photographs; one of the most moving is that of the gas chamber at Auschwitz. In the photograph a little girl is walking in front of her mother and doesn't know where she is going. The mother who walks behind her knows but there is nothing, absolutely nothing, she can do to prevent this tragedy. So in her helplessness, the mother performs the only act of love that is left to her. She places her hand over the little girl's eyes so she cannot see the approaching horror. As I gazed with others at the picture someone behind me cried out, "Oh, God, don't let this be all that there is. Somehow, somewhere, set things right!"

So here are some suggestions—minor but significant suggestions—to set things right. Two of them. First, for those of us who buy records and tapes I suggest that for every fifth one you would buy, don't. Take the cost of the record and give it to the needy, to a charity. Michael Jackson won't miss it. For those who are sports fans, for every four games you see, don't see the fifth one. Give the cost of the ticket to charity. Bobby Bonilla won't miss it.

And tell yourself, your friends, and your family what you're doing and why. You don't have to say you're under the judgment of the gospel, but if you do, you would be pretty accurate. Instead, you might mumble something about not being surprised.

The second suggestion is that as a family or a neighborhood you have an ongoing, communal charity such as Covenant House or Save the Children. Put an empty coffee can on the table and every member of your family or bridge club or neighborhood can drop some money into it. Celebrate when you count it and send it in.

These are easy suggestions, tokens really, but they're a beginning. They're a reminder of the criterion for salvation set out by this gospel. We know clearly the measurement used to separate the sheep from the goats. There'll be many surprises at Judgment Day, but no Christian should ever be surprised.

15

✟

Stewardship

(Mark 12:38-44)

Someone has nicely defined the difference between prosperity, recession, and depression. During prosperity, you are annoyed because the dog and the cat won't eat the expensive canned food you bought for them. In a recession, you are delighted that they *don't* eat the expensive canned food and hope they remain finicky until things get better. And in a depression you begin to look thoughtfully at the dog and cat.

Then there's the threefold category of givers. Some givers are like a piece of flint: to get anything out of them, you have to hammer at them morning, noon, and night, and even then you get only chips and sparks. Some givers are categorized as a sponge; to get anything out of them you've got to squeeze, and squeeze hard, because the more you squeeze, the more you get. And then there are those a who are like honeycomb: people who just overflow from their own sweetness.

Then there is the story of the teacher who asked the class why, in the parable of the Good Samaritan, the priest didn't go over and help the man by the wayside but just passed by. A little girl answered, "Because he saw that the man had *already* been robbed."

And, finally, this parable. There once was a man who had nothing. And God gave him ten apples. God gave three apples for food. The man ate the first three apples. God gave him another three apples to trade for shelter from the sun and rain. So he traded the second three apples for shelter from the sun and rain. And God gave him three apples to trade for clothing to cover his body, and so he traded the three apples for clothing to cover his body. And God gave him a tenth apple so he would have something to give back to God in gratitude for the other nine. And the man held up the tenth apple to examine it in admiration. It seemed larger and juicier than all the rest. He knew in his heart that this was the apple that God expected him to use as a gift of gratitude for the other nine, but the tenth apple did seem better than all the others, and he reasoned that God had all the other apples in the world, so the man ate the tenth apple and gave the core back to God.

All these stories are prompted by the Scriptures today, the stories of the prophet Elijah who was starving to death and the poor widow who shared her small substance with him, and the gospel's famous widow who put in her mite, all she had to live on. How can we not talk about money? But not in order to ask for it. It would be just my luck that someone's here this morning finally coming back to church after forty-four years and he gets a sermon about money, the very thing he left over way back then!

But, no, giving money is not our topic and never has been. Rather, our topic is broader. It's about money and Catholics all right, but it's about something much deeper religiously, something more profound, something that has to do with our spirituality as Catholics and so therefore something to reflect on together. But first, some data.

The text for this data comes from a *Wall Street Journal* article. It points out that United States Catholics are the wealthiest religious group in the entire country—and second to the wealthiest sociological group, Jews. The income of American Catholics averages $31,475. And yet—and here is the startling contrast—this wealthiest of all religious groups gives almost the least to religion, only 1 percent of its income. Catholics rank the third lowest of all Christian denominations in a field of hundreds. Catholic giving is a far cry, for example, from the 7 percent that Mormons give. Other independent studies have confirmed this fact and furthermore indicate that America's 55 million Roman Catholics contribute about half as much as they did twenty years ago, and that only one out of every five Catholic families gives anything at all, either to its parish or to its diocese.

The results are obvious in the daily newspaper reports that tell us of regular closings of Catholic institutions, parishes, and schools. You might recollect, for example, that in 1989 the archdiocese of Detroit closed 31 parishes because they just could not survive financially. Chicago is faced with a 28-million-dollar deficit. Two-thirds of its parishes are in debt. New York has all kinds of school closings. This scenario is repeated daily everywhere throughout the United States. All across this county two hundred elementary schools have closed for lack of funds, and half of the nation's Roman Catholic high schools as well. And this, ironically, when all of the independent and secular surveys show the consistent superiority of Catholic education in every category and all across the board.

All of this leaves a $65 *billion* shortfall in the last two decades for the Roman Catholic church in America. Last year the diocese of Albany, which is a typical diocese, took a survey and found that only one-third of its Catholic families support the church, and that third averages out to giving about six dollars a week to the parish and $1.50 a week to the diocese.

No one can operate, can survive, with those numbers.

All this raises a severe and obvious question: why do Roman Catholics, the wealthiest religious group in the nation, give almost the least amount to its religion? There are all kinds of theories and you may have some thoughts of your own. Here are some theories of others. Some reason that the average church-goer is younger today, which means they have no history, no pioneering spirit like their ancestors who built the churches and schools and had a deep, personal, vested interest in their success. Or perhaps the young are addicted to consumerism on the one hand and hemmed in by a recession on the other. Their thinking and their allegiance are just not geared to the church.

Others say, "Well, maybe," but they think withholding money is the only way some people have to vote their dissatisfaction with the church and its policies. Or a variation says that with such large parishes in many places there is no practical participation. If you don't have a sense of ownership, community, determination of what goes on, or even accountability—then, why bother? After all, where does the money go? What happens to it?

These and other reasons may have some validity, but the issue really goes deeper than all of them. I think the rock-bottom reason for Catholic stinginess is basically a religious one: unlike the Mormons or some Protestant denominations, *we lack a religious tradition of stewardship.* We lack a sense of that tradition that sees giving as a natural and basic responsibility of faith. That notion seems so foreign to us. Very few Catholics—including ourselves—ever even think of structuring their giving into their household budget as a part of their faith commitment. This connection is never made. For some reason it's not in our thinking, our consciousness. Faith and money is a non-issue with us. Our understanding is that church is church, and money is money, and one has nothing to do with the other.

But that's our lack, for the issue is real. The issue, the stewardship question, is this: what does following Jesus Christ demand of us regarding our use of the goods of this created world? Discipleship should beget stewardship. Discipleship asks, for whom do we use our gifts of time, talent, and treasure? It reminds us that what we have is not what we own. We in fact don't "own" anything. We are merely stewards of creation for a while. All of us, sooner or later, will have to surrender what we have. Meanwhile, we have been given a solemn trust on which we must make a return. We should not pollute our gifts, cut down rain forests, destroy the environment, because they are not ours. To despoil the earth is a contradiction of the gospel. To horde our money is to be on the negative side of the parable of the man who hid his talent in the ground and made no return. The Book of Proverbs' saying, "Honor the Lord with your wealth, with first fruits of all your produce" is a gospel attitude. There is a connection between faith and the money we have. We too are stewards of that and must make a return to the Lord.

But if we break the connection between faith and money or never even make it, then we have no religious sense of stewardship. Giving to God the core and not the apple is the result. And Catholics, as the *Journal* tells us, evidently have given and continue to give a lot of apple cores. Somehow, we who built the orphanages, schools, churches, and hospitals when we were poor have held back when we became the wealthiest religious group in America. We've lost sight of the fact that faith tells us that we are but servants of the world, managers of our money, trustees of our gifts—all of which were given to us but for a time and to share. That conviction is part of our religion and a condition of discipleship. It's what we call stewardship.

The Elijah and widow's mite stories are ancient reminders of our stewardship. Whatever the reason Catholics don't give, the basic one seems to come down to a failure to connect faith and money, to figure giving into our annual budget, to train our children in a posture of servanthood, of being caretakers-for-a-while of this earth and all they have. To use their gifts wisely. Getting around to the notion of stewardship is getting around to a faith that works.

16

+

Love of Self

(Mark 12:28-34)

The truths of the love of God and the love of neighbor are to be found in Jesus' ancestral Scripture, but he was the first to connect them and make one dependent on the other; to make them two sides, as it were, of the same spiritual coin.

What sometimes is forgotten, however, is that Jesus put a third term there which is the foundation and the beginning of the other two. Notice he said, "You shall love God with your whole heart, soul, and mind, and you shall love your neighbor." But the measurement for both is *"as yourself."* And so it would seem that if we do not start there and love ourselves we might find it quite difficult and perhaps impossible to connect to God and neighbor.

Most of you have heard of John Bradshaw, the author-psychologist on television. He speaks of the "inner child of the past" which, if battered physically or emotionally, will affect who and what we are today in a negative way. Although he falls into the usual pelagianism—meaning he thinks the human beings are ultimately their own corrective and answer if they try hard enough—he offers us some examples that we can relate to the gospel. In his book *Homecoming: Reclaiming and Championing Your Inner Child,* he gives these instances:

> When Maximillian's girlfriend ends their six-month relationship he feels suicidal. He believes that his worth depends on her loving him. Maximillian has no self-worth, which is engendered from within; he has "others' worth" which depends on other people. And, of course, if all that depends on other people, most of Maximillian's energy has to go to erecting a facade so that other people will both affirm and love him.

Our gospel commentary is that with all that energy going into protecting a self he really doesn't love, there's not much energy left to love God or neighbor. He in fact *is* loving them as he loves himself—which is to say, not very much.

> Ophelia Oliphant demands that her husband buy her a Mercedes. She also insists on keeping their membership in the River Valley Country Club. The Oliphants are heavily in debt. They live from paycheck to paycheck. They spend enormous amounts of energy juggling creditors and fashioning an image of upper-class wealth. Ophelia believes that her self-esteem depends on maintaining the proper image. She has no inner sense of self.

Again, our gospel commentary would be that with no inner sense of self she cannot have a real sense of God or neighbor. People with no sense of self find it hard to love another.

That sense of having no self-worth, as has often been observed, comes early. It's put into people when they are young, when they are physically, sexually, emotionally, or verbally abused. Or when they are abandoned physically or emotionally. John Bradshaw himself was abandoned by his alcoholic father when he was about two years old. He recounts that this abandonment came back to affect him many years later when he went on a trip with his daughter, a very well-adjusted young woman. He relates that when they were on a cruise visiting the capitals of Europe the daughter suggested that they make a little side trip and take the train and visit some inland places. She thought the idea delightful, but he immediately went into a panic. On reflection he discovered that his panic problem was that if they took the train, suppose it was late and they didn't get back in time and they missed the boat and it sailed off without them? He had already been abandoned by his father and he didn't want to take the chance of being abandoned again, of being left, literally and figuratively, alone.

Abandonment, physical and emotional, happens among the affluent also. This is seen in a large survey on family life two years ago. The main question asked of hundreds of thousands was, "What is the most critical value in your whole life? What really means most to you? What's on the top of the scale?" Ninety-seven percent of the people gave the identical answer: family life. But, they added, they feel badly that they don't have enough time to spend together. That was the common lament. So they were asked another question: "If you got an opportunity for a better job that offered more money and prestige, but would take you away even more from your family so that you would spend even less time with them, would you take it?" Eighty percent said yes! That's called addictive behavior: choosing a priority you know is harmful, in this case, to the greater priority of cherished human relationships. But, in any case, the child's interpretation is that "if I am worth less of your time, I am worthless." It's an easy and accurate jump. That child's going to find it hard to feel self-esteem, to love, to trust.

So it would seem we're in a quandary. If we are to love God and neighbor as ourselves but—not through our own fault—do not love ourselves, are we doomed forever to not fulfilling the two great commandments? Are we lost? Is there no reclamation? Can we find healing for the abuse and restoration of the poor image? In short, can we learn to love ourselves—can we be freed to love ourselves—so that we can truly move to our heart's desire of genuinely loving others and loving God?

Jesus, who joined the two Commandments, is compassionate; he does not leave us orphaned. He constantly offers us three gifts to get us back to the knowledge of the worth with which we were created. The first gift Jesus offers us is forgiveness. And when I say that, you immediately think, "Of course. He forgives our sins." And you think of things like lying and cheating and stealing, and so forth. But Jesus offers forgiveness for something far more basic than those things. He goes right to the center, offering to forgive us for hating ourselves, which is often why we get into those other sins to begin with. And that self-hate is a terrible sin because God didn't make us like that: hateful. God made all things and "saw that they were good." If we are made to the very image and likeness of God, if through baptism we were called "beloved sons and daughters," if Jesus so loved us as to give his life for us, if we are no longer servants but friends, then what more affirmation can we have or desire? At the center we are good. At the center we are loved. To hate oneself is to reject the truth about ourselves, to reject the God who first loved us. That's why self-hate needs forgiveness badly, and that's the first reclamation that Jesus offers.

The second gift Jesus offers is simply a variation of his first offer of forgiveness: it is conversion. Again, we think of converting from vice to virtue, from darkness to light. That is not so here. The conversion Jesus offers is more fundamental, more basic. It is the conversion to our own lovableness. After forgiving our self-hate, Jesus offers us a new vision of ourselves, a turning around to seeing ourselves as we truly are: children of God. It's the moment of "amazing grace." I once was blind to the God within me, but now I see. I once was lost to self-hate, but now am found in love. That's conversion.

The third gift Jesus offers us is his enduring presence and acceptance, his persistent habit of reading the heart and not the face. And in an advertising-laden culture that glorifies the external image, this is no small thing. He offers us memories to live by: the memory of him literally touching the disfigured leper, the unclean woman, the greedy tax collector, the wretched thief. He offers us the memories of his many meals with the marginal, rejected, and disenfranchised. How, then, could he not look on us with love? How could he not see past our disfigurements and early scars and not reach out daily to touch us? In a word, he offers us his friendship, through thick and thin, for better or for worse, in sickness and in health—till death and beyond. He simply sees beyond the surface and loves what he sees.

Let me end with a story from the Franciscan nun, Sister Jose Hobday, one she tells that happened at Thanksgiving when she was a child.

My mother loved older people. When we were children she used to send us off with gifts for them: a plate of cookies, freshly baked bread, Easter eggs in a basket. She was always looking out for older people.

One day she sent me to visit an old woman named Mrs. Casey. It was a very difficult mission for a child because Mrs. Casey had cancer and as a result she had no nose. Her face was bandaged from her eyes to her mouth. Her disease also caused a bad smell. Visiting Mrs. Casey was a real ordeal, particularly since my mother expected me to sit and talk and spend some time with her. After a couple of visits I told my mother to have one of my brothers visit Mrs. Casey. I didn't want to see her any more. That was all my mother needed to make sure I kept going over to see Mrs. Casey. I dreaded it every time, but I always sat down and visited like my mother wanted.

One day in November my mother announced she was inviting Mrs. Casey over for Thanksgiving dinner. I objected, saying that her smell would ruin my dinner. My mother told me I was going to have to adjust because Mrs. Casey didn't have any place else to go. I thought about the baked turkey and the pumpkin pies and my all-time Thanksgiving favorite, sweet potatoes. Not wanting to miss any of it, I told my mother I would sit at the other end of the table. But on Thanksgiving Day my mother sat me directly across from Mrs. Casey.

I kept my eyes down and tried to be polite, but it was difficult, especially when the sweet potatoes started coming around. They were filled with marshmallows and brown sugar, just the way I like them. But as the sweet potatoes came to my brother, he took two. That was against the rule in our house. You took one of anything until you were sure everyone else had one. But he thought he was being smart. He could see I was the last one being served and wouldn't get any if he took two. He also knew that with all the company present, I couldn't object as surely I would have done otherwise.

When the sweet potato platter got to Mrs. Casey, she counted the number of people and saw that I wouldn't get any, so she passed it on without taking any. When it got to me there was still one left. I felt terrible. I took it. And I'm glad to say I had the good grace to cut it in half and offer a portion to Mrs. Casey. When I did that, a strange thing happened. She didn't smell any more. She looked like a lovely person. She smiled back at me, took the potato, and we had a great Thanksgiving dinner.

Later, when I learned about the life of St. Francis, I came to see this Thanksgiving encounter as similar to the conversion experience he had when he embraced the leper. I learned never to let a scar on someone's outside, no matter how ugly, keep me from seeing the beauty on the inside.

If a disciple of Jesus could reach such a conclusion, how much more could Jesus himself? He never lets a scar on someone's outside or inside keep him from seeing the beauty on the inside. Never. So, then, that's where self-love begins: in the knowledge that we are loved fully and unconditionally by God. Knowing that, experiencing that, is the basis for loving others—God and neighbor—as myself.

17

✝

The Mother-in-Law's Restoration

(Mark 1:29-39)

There's a hurting and a healing theme in today's gospel, which tells us the story of Peter's ill mother-in-law. But the hurt is not just concerned with her illness back then. It has an unintended contemporary ring. By that I mean that feminine consciousness might be hurt, offended, by the whole episode in the first place. Why? Because, on the surface, what do you have? You have a group of hungry men come into the house. But it so happens that the woman of the house is ill. So they tell Jesus about her and he goes over and cures her. And then the very next sentence says, "And immediately she got up and waited on them." How about that? Does that arouse the suspicion that the men folk could not even get their own lunch and so they prevailed upon Jesus to work a cure so they could have a woman wait on them? Is there a battle of the sexes issue here: men are served and women do the serving? A woman's place is in the home?

So it would seem, but, actually, that's reading a modern agenda into this episode. Nothing was further from the gospel writer's mind—in this case, St. Mark—and it needn't be in ours. What the gospel writer was saying in this story of hurt and healing was something near and dear to his heart: that when Jesus Christ touches you and you become his disciple, then you immediately enter into service. That's the nature and the power of love. Discipleship is not about freedom or power or authority. Discipleship is about lowly, selfless service in the name of God. That's the message here.

If you want another gospel writer's variation on the same theme, go to St. John's account of the Last Supper. At that supper, you well recall, Jesus put on a towel and knelt down and washed the feet of his disciples. And then he said pointedly, echoing Mark's gospel, "You know what I have done? You call me Lord and Master, and so I am. And if I, Lord and Master, have washed your feet, so must you wash each other's feet." Thus the lesson once more: those who are touched by Jesus, genuinely touched, those who respond to him, automatically imitate him by entering into loving service. So this is the meaning behind Peter's mother-in-law's cure. She, along with her son-in-law, was touched by Jesus. She, like her son-in-law, became a disciple. She, like him, also served.

But let us move beyond that woman and that era and look at our own hurts, our own losses. As the poem says:

O Savior, Christ, our woes dispel,
For some are sick and some are sad;
And some have never loved thee well,
And some have lost the love they had.

We've all lost some love. We've lost a lot of things: innocence, childhood, relationships, jobs, health, marriages, children, self-respect, youth, vigor—all of these and more. Life is full of unnecessary and necessary losses and, consequently, pain and suffering. Is there also healing? We are like a fevered mother-in-law. Is there a Jesus nearby to restore us?

There is a restoration but perhaps not in the sense that we think, not in the sense of a sudden and miraculous cure that makes everything as it was before.

There is restoration, rather, in the sense that we have the opportunity *not* to have it as it was before. That is to say, we have a chance in our hurt for healing on a much deeper level, a healing toward that wholeness that leads us to God, a healing that leaves us scarred but different from what we were. Let me share with you five principles that lead to that restoration.

The first principle is this: We must search for meaning in the pain and suffering that comes to us. If we are preoccupied in running away *from* pain, we are not likely to discover the meaning that might be found in running *with* pain. Not that we ever seek pain out or that we revel in suffering. But when pain is present, there is also a call to discover a new facet of life in ourselves. It is not enough for us to recognize that we share common brokenness with all the other people who are hurting, and it's not enough simply to tell our tale of woes. It is only when somehow our pain is internalized in a meaningful way that it has the possibility of bringing us to some new place in life. Suffering may seem to break us, but unless our lives are not only broken, but broken *into*, then we shed tears "that turn no mill," as the poet says. We don't have redemptive suffering in our lives. Suffering must move us to a different place than where we have been up to this point. We have to discover its meaning for us.

The second principle is that all of us in our pain and suffering need help. St. Paul is a good example. Remember when he was knocked off his horse on the road to Damascus? He hears a voice saying, "Get up and go into the city and there you will be told what you are to do." And in the city he meets a little man named Ananias, who cures Paul of his blindness and introduces him to the faith. All of us need an Ananias, a spiritual guide, a friend or, as the English put it, a soul-friend. And in turn we have to play Ananias to others. But we all need help toward restoration. Pain is a communal adventure.

The third principle is this: we need our past. This is often dismissed or ignored, but it's not wise to do so. St. Paul's change of direction in his life was not an invitation to abandon or deny his past. Rather it was a call to search for the connection between what he had been and what he had become, between where he was and where he was going. We need our past as a guidepost to our journey. We preserve this wisdom every time we sing

> Amazing Grace, how sweet the sound
> That saved a wretch like me.
> I once was lost, but now am found
> Was blind but now I see.

It's only when we remember our wretchedness, lostness, and blindness that we can celebrate the grace of what we have become. We need to remember the health, the gain, and the virtue—and the loss, the death, and the sin—to see the road we've traveled and the patient working of grace. It may be painful, but we need our past to get past pain—and to measure our progress.

Fourth, if it is true that we need our past to see where we have been, it is also true that we don't need the past to keep us there and prevent us from connecting to the future. I mean, there is a past that we not only remember, but we remember with terrible and paralyzing guilt so that we do not pass through it, grow through it, but get stuck in it instead. This is especially true in the area of moral pain. This is the cry: years ago I was unfaithful, had an abortion, embezzled, was alcoholic, abusive to my family, and so on. Years ago I did this or that horrid thing. And that horrid thing just hangs there and we can't forgive ourselves. The memory of the deed is ever present, an ongoing pain that is not redemptive but constricting; it goes nowhere except ever deeper within. It provides no bridge to the future but is a dead weight to the past. The healing that moves us beyond this is to recall the words of the mystics, "God is greater than your own accusing heart. God is greater than your own accusing heart." That must become the mantra that moves us ahead. It's the rock-bottom conviction that turned a Saul into a Paul, a Simon into Peter, Magdalen into an apostle, Augustine into a mystic, and scores of other sinners who found God's mercy to be greater than their sin and so traveled forward with their new revelation into glory.

The fifth and final principle is a kind of summary. The question we have to ask about the pain and hurt that comes to us is this: "What is the weeping asking of me?" That is the critical question. "What is the weeping asking of me?" How can it move me from one place to another? To a fuller, more whole person? To the saint God created me to be? What is its message, its meaning?

St. Mark's message was that Peter's mother-in-law was sick and hurt. She had no idea of unexpected company that day and dearly wished there would be none, since understandably she was not in the mood for entertaining. But as she lay on her bed wondering what her sickness could mean, she received unexpected help. A healer came into her life. Afterwards, she never forgot the time she was sick and tired. It was a painful experience, but there's no denying something had happened to her. She grew into something she never dreamed possible. She became a disciple of the Messiah, not just any old disciple but one who did service with sensitivity and compassion, for she knew that was the ultimate meaning of her suffering.

18

+

Decision Time

(John 12:20-33)

We're often put off by the gospel, especially John's gospel. Take, for example, the one we just heard. A couple of Greeks seek an audience with Jesus. They find Philip and ask him to arrange an interview. Philip teams up with Andrew and they both approach Jesus. So far, so good. Sounds like a typical chain-of-command process. Apparently, then, Philip and Andrew tell Jesus there's a couple of Greeks who want to talk with him—and after that, we're lost.

We're lost because Jesus launches into a monologue that has nothing whatever to do with the matter at hand. He doesn't say yes or no to his disciples. He doesn't say he's too busy or not now. Completely out of context he says, "Now is the Son of Man to be glorified." And he goes on to talk about a grain of wheat needing to die before it lives again in another way, about losing one's life in order to gain it, about being shaken in his innermost depths to the extent of asking his Father to save him from an impending ordeal, namely, his death.

The two disciples must have turned and looked at each other wondering, What kind of an answer was that? and What do we do with these impatient Greeks? They had received a non-answer. And they were right. As I said, Jesus' reply doesn't fit the context. That is, until you know what the gospel writer is assuming; namely, that we know that Jesus is in a state of mind, that he is in fact preoccupied, that he is at this point in his life distracted. For the fact of the matter is that he, sensing impending doom, has arrived at a decision time in his life and he is struggling with whether to flee it or face it. And so, almost as if he didn't hear his two disciples' request, he pours out his fears, his feelings, his heart. Something is weighing heavily on his mind, more critical issues than an audience request. He is struggling with a weighty decision and, as we know, he will repeat that struggle in the Garden of Gethsemane.

So this is the reverie the disciples have interrupted and now we understand Jesus' reply, which was no reply to them, but which is meant to be a running commentary to us. Will he flee and save his life, or will he lose his life and thereby save it? Will *we* flee and save our lives, or will *we* lose our lives for his sake and find them? He is being called to be a grain of wheat that must die before it can live. Can he accept that? *We* are called to be a grain of wheat that must die before *we* can truly live. Can we accept that?

Jesus concludes that he must. There is no other way to salvation. The one who saves his life will lose it, the one who loses it for God's sake will save it. And God is all for Jesus. That's the path he chooses, and it becomes the spiritual wisdom he leaves us. And now, in the form of this gospel, it also becomes the question that challenges us. We are asked to choose: to live or to die to self?

Let me share two modern stories of such decisions. There is a man named Sundar who is still alive, born in India, a member of the Sikh religion. He became a convert to Christianity and decided to stay in India to be a missionary and bear witness to Jesus. One late afternoon Sundar was traveling on foot high in the Himalaya mountains with a Buddhist monk. It was bitter cold and the night was coming on. The monk warned that they were in danger of freezing to death if they did not reach the monastery before the darkness fell.

Well, it happened that as they crossed over a narrow path above a steep cliff, they heard a cry for help. And deep down in the ravine a man had fallen, and he lay wounded. His leg was broken and he couldn't walk. So the monk warned Sundar, "Do not stop. God has brought this man to his fate. He must work it out by himself. That is the tradition. Let us hurry on before we perish." But Sundar replied, "It is my tradition now that God has brought me here to help my brother. I cannot abandon him." So the monk set off through the snow, which had started to fall heavily. But Sundar climbed down to where the wounded man was. Since the man had a broken leg, Sundar took a blanket from his knapsack and made a sling out of it. He got the man into it and hoisted him on his back and began the painful and arduous climb back up the path. After a long time, drenched with perspiration, he finally got back to the path, struggling to make his way through the increasingly heavily falling snow. It was dark now and he had all he could do to find the path. But he persevered and although faint from fatigue and overheated from exertion he finally saw the lights of the monastery.

Then he nearly stumbled and fell. Not from weakness. He stumbled over an object lying in the path. He bent down on one knee and brushed the snow from the body of the monk who had frozen to death within sight of the monastery. And there, kneeling on one knee in the snow, he said aloud to himself the Scripture we heard today: The one who would save his life will lose it and the one who loses his life for my sake will find it. And he understood what Jesus meant and was glad that he had decided to "lose his life" for another.

Years later, when Sundar had his own disciples, they asked him this question: "Master, what is life's most difficult task?" And Sundar replied, "To have no burden to carry." By that he meant not only the burden of challenge, but he also meant the burden of decision, that no one is really human, really alive, really a disciple of Christ unless that person at some time in life makes the decision to lose his or her life and so to live, to become, in the gospel's figure of speech, the grain of wheat. To prefer God to self.

Another variation of the gospel theme is found in the movie *Rainman.* You recall that Tom Cruise plays a selfish, hustling salesman named Charlie Babbitt, and Dustin Hoffman plays his older autistic brother Raymond who had been institutionalized. Charlie Babbitt didn't even know he had an older brother, much less an autistic one, and the only reason he acknowledges him now is that the father had died and left three million dollars to autistic Raymond and an old '49 Buick to hotshot Charlie. Charlie spends most of his time moving in on poor Raymond to manipulate and cheat him out of the inheritance. After all, how would a guy like that know what to do with all that money? But in the course of the movie, against his will, Charlie begins to care for Raymond. Before he knows it, for the first time in his life, he is thinking more of another than of himself. Slowly he begins to die to self and live for Raymond. At one point he has to make a decision to do so, very much like our preoccupied Jesus. He becomes a different, a whole person. Or, as we would say in religious language, he becomes redeemed. He lost his life for Raymond's sake only to find it for his own.

So, all along the line, this gospel, so strange in its development, suddenly takes on meaning. We are asked to stand in the long line of Jesus, Sundar, and Charlie Babbitt. We can't avoid making decisions—none of us can do that—we can only make them unconsciously. We can let them slide without much thought into self-serving actions. This gospel pulls us out of such preoccupations and makes us face what we would not like to face: Who *are* we? What means so much to us that we'll die for it? Who or what is larger than ourselves? What must we let go of in order to grow? For whose sake will we give our lives and save them? Or will we desperately try to save our lives, only to wind up losing them?

It's decision time. That's what this gospel is basically about and why it found its way into our tradition. We are being challenged to give an answer to life's fundamental question: which is not Hamlet's "To be or not to be," but Jesus' "To love or not to love."

19

✝

Cross, Crown, and Commitment

(Mark 10:35-45)

The pastor of a small congregation was being prosletyzed by some energetic missionaries. He listened for a while and then said to them: "Gentlemen, look. I have a proposal that will settle this. I have here a glass of poison. If you will drink this poison and remain alive I will join your church—and not only myself, but my entire congregation. But if you won't drink the poison, well, then, I can only conclude that you are false ministers of the gospel because you do not trust that your Lord would not let you perish." This put the missionaries in a bind, so they went off to a corner to put their heads together and they said, "What on earth are we going to do?" So finally, after a while, they decided. They came back and approached the minister and said, "Tell you what. We've got a plan. You drink the poison and we'll raise you from the dead!"

That story, believe it or not, is a variation of the story we heard in today's gospel. In the gospel there are two apostles, James and John—elsewhere dubbed Sons of Thunder because they were a fairly hot-headed pair—asking for the reward of special seating at Jesus' right and left hand, but without the risk. They were asking for the crown without the cross, the status without the integrity, the image without the likeness, the fulfillment without the commitment. But commitment, as you know, by definition includes the cross. They're two sides to the same reality. If you commit to fidelity, the Open Marriage and Alternate Lifestyle people will get after you. If you commit to honesty, the dishonest people will give you grief. If you commit to truth, the liars will tell lies about you. If you commit to chastity the media will give you Calvin Klein. If you commit to ethics, someone will blow the whistle on you. In brief, if you make a commitment of any kind, the cross is never far behind. The two apostles didn't understand that; they wanted all the crowns without the cross, all the company without the commitments. That's why Jesus caught them up short and asked somewhat sarcastically, "Can you drink of the cup of suffering? Can you make commitments and all that goes with them? That's the only way to a significant position in my kingdom."

The ancient gospel, as you know, never lets the incident lay there in the past. It always jumps up to the present and confronts us. The question it raises for each generation is, "What commitments ought we, the modern-day James and John, make if we want to sit at the right and left hands of Jesus? And are we willing to take the cross that goes with them?" In search of an answer I suggest five areas that we might consider, areas that call for both commitment and cross.

The first area is the commitment to love God. I know that sounds banal, but think about it. I mean that the commitment to love God involves time. We must give God time. A professor friend of mine has a very wonderful marriage and he often remarks that people comment on the closeness he and his wife have and he always tells them the secret of it. He says, "Twenty-two years ago when I was a young professor, busy teaching and writing and running around the country giving lectures and speaking, I received a sabbatical year. Well, my wife and I decided to spend it in Paris. For the first time in my life, I had large chunks of unprogrammed time to use in any way I chose. Our children were both in school for the first time, so my wife and I went off and spent half-days together, walking through the beautiful city or sitting on the bank of the Seine River. We had been married fifteen years, but it was as if we had just discovered each other. Ever since, we have valued the time we have together. We have struggled to create time when our schedules denied it. And being together has produced intimacy." It's the same with God. As every great and busy saint from Augustine to Mother Teresa knows, they have to commit time to God. The cross is struggling to create time for God when your schedule would deny it. The crown is God himself.

The second commitment is to put people, to put relationships, first. Again, that sounds simple enough but in fact, because of our cultural programming, we do not do that. A case in point: in yesterday's paper there was in the family section a lament that very few parents sit and read aloud to their children these days. One commentator, remarking on her California survey, wrote, "In these four hundred to five hundred thousand dollar homes, the researchers found only two parents who read aloud regularly more than once a week to their children. By contrast," she adds, "many parents resort to popping a video into the machine and placing kids in front of the tube."

Psychiatrist Thomas Connell remarks that there is no substitute not only for reading skills, but for the intimacy engendered by sitting in the lap of mom and dad. These are memorable and warm moments for every child, the apex of relationship—where they are taught that they are special and loved. And yet many of our children, according to the surveys, never experience this. As Dr. Connell says, "In today's post-literate culture, you now have a society where Mommy and Daddy who read to a child is not entirely an anomaly, but these people are bucking the major trends. In two-career families the practice of reading aloud to children can become a casualty of maddeningly tight schedules. People just have such frenetic lifestyles. Children are getting short-shrifted."

But then, Jim Trelise, the national guru-author-advocate of reading aloud to children, responds, "Well, if there's little time for this sort of thing in the lives of parents today, why do we have more shopping malls open more hours than ever before? Why do the number of video stores now outnumber public libraries five to one? If they don't have time to read to their children, why do they have time to go shopping or to rent videos?"

When you bring home the question like that into our everyday lives, you can see the power behind asking about our commitments to our deepest relationships: the children we love so much. The cross is rerouting our priorities in order to put people—little people—first. The crown is a child nestled in your lap.

The third area of commitment to be challenged is our desire to be holy. We say, of course, we want to be holy—whatever that means. But it means something far less complicated than we think. The simplest definition of what it means to be holy is to learn not to fear one another. When we learn not to fear public opinion so we can be ourselves, not to fear one another so we can entrust our most secret selves to him or her, not to fear betrayal so we can let our words tumble out without measurement, explanation, or apology—then we are holy. To be committed to be holy is to be committed to not being afraid so that we can be intimate. The cross side of such commitment is, of course, exposure to vulnerability and therefore hurt. The crown side is growth.

The fourth commitment is inspired by Mother Teresa's advice: "We can't do the big things, you and I. We're not capable of them. But do the little things faithfully." Being committed to the little things—the smile smiled, the courtesy rendered, the dinner prepared, the hug exploded, the birthday remembered, the flowers sent, the compliment given—is a form of holiness within our grasp. The cross is to keep on forgetting self. The crown is making life more pleasant, endurable, and joyous.

The final area of commitment suggested is perhaps the hardest of all. It is the serious commitment to trying to let God love us. Oh, we're very good at trying to love other people and we sincerely try to love God. But to open ourselves to the rich, total outpouring of *God's* love—that's something else again. I mean, we know how sinful we are, how unworthy, how shamed. It's better to give all the active energy in working at loving others—and thereby deflecting the attention away from ourselves—than to be the passive, restful recipient and object of love, especially God's love. It seems we find it hard to tolerate the fact that God, knowing what God knows, can love us.

All right, then, picture this scene in your mind's eye. It is the recreation room of a California retirement facility. Four women are playing bridge and chatting and keeping an eye on the flow of people in and out of the area. And soon an elderly man walks into the room. They all recognize him as a newcomer and they all perk up. One of the women says, "Hello, there. You're new here, aren't you?" He smiles and replies that indeed he is. He has just arrived this morning. The second woman says, "And where did you live before you moved in?" He says, " I was just released from San Quentin, where I spent the last twenty years." A third woman perks up at this and asks, "Oh, is that so? What were you in for?" He says, "I murdered my wife." The fourth woman sits up in the chair and smiles and says, "Oh, then you're single?"

Is it too much to say that God is like a witty and foolish woman who will have her man no matter what? No, that's not too much to say. After all, Jesus said God was like an unwitty and foolish old man who himself ran down to embrace and kiss a wayward son. Jesus said God was like a stupid if not demented herdsman who would abandon ninety-nine sheep to search for one lost sheep, which would have been replaced in a short time anyway. In other words, after all of our sins and transgressions are revealed, God still sits up and takes notice and says in his most flirtatious manner, "Oh, then you're single?" Yes, he'll have us, no matter what. And so to believe that and to be committed to let down our defenses so God can love us is our toughest decision. True, the cross is surrendering pride, but the crown is gaining God.

Back to James and John. They wanted the crown, the privileges, the reward. They wanted, I suppose, Jesus himself, but they did not want his cross, his cup, his way. They didn't want the cost of commitment to him. And Jesus replies in essence, you can't have the one without the other. For us, as we said, this gospel asks about *our* commitments and we've tried to share in what areas those commitments might be. Certainly there are other areas, but the commitment to love God, to put relationships first, to be holy, to be faithful in little things, and to let God love us—surely these are among the most primary commitments in our lives. They all involve the cross. None offers a short cut. Each carries a penalty. But together they make up the Kingdom of God and our place in it.

20

✝

The Environmental Sabbath

(Matthew 6:25-29)

A man relates this story:

On a kayaking trip in the Apostle Islands in northern Wisconsin, my wife and I were talking to our guide as we ate our lunch on a remote beach. I mentioned how unusual it was to have no television, no newspapers, and no radio. "In fact," I said, "it's going to be strange to return home and find out what's happening in the real world." No one spoke for a few minutes. Then, without taking his eyes from the horizon, the guide commented, "I assume that's what you came *here* for."

That little story is an introduction to our special theme this weekend, which is our Environmental Sabbath. There are two parts to our comments: one is a litany, and the other is a religious challenge. The litany is not a litany of the saints as we might expect in church, but a litany of all too familiar statistics that are so astronomical that most of us can't fit them into our heads, but we mention them in the hope they might fit into our hearts.

Humanity has added 5.5 billion tons of carbon to the atmosphere in 1988 through fossil fuel combustion, and another 2.5 billion through deforestation. We have increased the amount of carbon dioxide in the air about 25 percent in the last century and undoubtedly it will increase twice as much in the next. In 1988 NASA's study of the global temperature records of the last century shows a gradual, long-term warming consistent with the models of the greenhouse effect. The five warmest years, as we can testify from experience, have all fallen in this decade.

More than 150 million people will get skin cancer in the United States alone over the next eighty years if nothing is done to save the ozone layer. In Canada some 20,000 lakes have been imperiled by acid rain. Nearly two billion people have inadequate drinking water. To date, according to the Environmental Protection Agency, more than 700 chemicals have been detected in United States drinking water. Eighty-eight percent of the newspapers that you and I will read this weekend have come from 500 thousand trees cut down in our country. These are the 88 percent that are not recycled. More than 22 billion pounds of hazardous waste were released or disposed of by the industries of the United States in 1987. The EPA estimates that 80 percent of the landfills now in operation will be close to capacity in twenty years. Due in part to the intense use of toxins in our country, the rate of cancer is rising by 2 percent each year. We are cutting down rain forests that took several hundred million years to evolve, the very lungs of our planet, at the rate of one football field of forest every second. We are losing over eighteen billion tons of topsoil each year, and are quickly running out of usable farm land. We are 5 percent of the world's population, but our cars use 26 percent of the world's oil, and our flush toilets and pesticides are ruining the ground water. We inject 82 billion tons of toxic waste every year into Earth's bloodstream. Biologists estimate that we are causing the extinction of 20,000 plant and animal species every year, one species every thirty minutes. We are extinguishing them forever.

As I said, I have difficulty with that litany of huge and mind-boggling numbers and it all sounds so alarmist—until you realize that in fact there is truth here, and a truth that we can observe. There *is* measurable damage to the environment. We can see it in the crawling desert and the blighted trees in upper New York State. That we may soon run out of ground water is quite possible and even probable. We have landfill trouble because we argue over incinerators. The local hospitals will tell us of the rise in skin cancer. Plant and animal species *have* disappeared and more are on the endangered list. We are warned not to eat the contaminated fish from certain nearby waters.

Is this what we have to bequeath to our children and grand-children, an uninhabitable planet? Something must be done. In the short space of time we have, our small contribution to "what must be done" is to share two insights that underpin the theme of the Environmental Sabbath. We can start, first of all, by learning to see ourselves not as apart *from* nature, but as a part *of* nature. As someone said, we are Earth's consciousness. After all, Earth is a living organism. It has its bloodstream in the rivers. It maintains its life through forests, air, and oxygen. We are part of all that, the brains of Mother Nature, if you will. We are not separate from nature. We are a part of it. We live and breathe and move in its rhythms. We share identical chemicals, molecules, and genes. There was a time when Americans understood that. Back in 1854 the Indian Chief Seattle purportedly wrote a letter to President Franklin Pierce that expresses the same insight. Among the many things he wrote in this famous letter is this sentence: "Whatever befalls Earth befalls the sons of Earth. Man did not weave the web of life; he is merely a strand in it. Whatever he does to the web, he does to himself."

The second insight—and the reason why we of a faith community celebrate the Environmental Sabbath today—is that we have in fact religious roots for a different view of nature and our relationship to it. The roots are three. First, we can return to the ancient Benedictine tradition of reverence for Earth. St.

Benedict in the fourth century farmed Earth with great respect and taught his monks to do the same. "To labor and to pray" remains the motto of the Benedictines. Prayer and work went together. A sense of being God's steward was the ideal. One did not dominate Earth; one worked with it. Or there's our Franciscan tradition of the twelfth century. St. Francis is the patron saint of ecology and we all know of his communion with nature. His "Brother Sun and Sister Moon" is more than poetry; it is a reality we need to recapture.

The second root is to see the environmental issue as primarily a moral one. Pope John Paul II said last year, "The ecological crisis is a moral crisis." We have to assume moral responsibility for Earth. It's a matter of conscience, a matter of religion.

Lastly, the third root—and this is the hardest of all—we have to change our lifestyles. Pervasive and consumerist advertising is so powerful and omnipresent that to change our habits of consumption and our throw-away mentality will border on the heroic. Our love affair with the car, for example, has made a widow of public transportation and one day its pollution will make widows of us all. Our stimulated need to overbuild, overeat, overuse has to be recognized for what it is: a deadly borrowing on our children's future. But change we must if there is to be a future.

The Environmental Sabbath, then, is a religious occasion meant to recall these truths: We are a part of nature. We live in relationship with the mighty organism of which we are a part. We need to retap those religious traditions of ours that held us accountable for our stewardship of Earth and therefore confronted us with a moral position. We need the asceticism of our tradition that helps us see that less is more; that we owe it to other people with whom we share this planet to spread more evenly the bounties of a healthy Earth. And surely, as we said, we owe a fertile and healthy Earth to our descendants.

All right. Perhaps we need to end our serious reflections with a light story that makes a heavy point concerning the environment. It's the story of a man in a small southern city who bought a bus ticket to go to Macon, Georgia. And he waited and waited and checked his watch. The bus should be arriving soon. So he wandered about a bit and his attention was diverted to a large scale that promised to tell not only one's age, but also one's name and any other pertinent information about the person being weighed. So, naturally curious, he stepped on the scale and put in his quarter and a slip came out. And on the slip it said, "Your name is Harry Harrison. You live in Sparta, Georgia. You weigh 197 pounds. You are seventeen pounds overweight. You are on your way to visit your sister in Macon. The bus to Macon has been delayed. Have a nice day." He was surprised and obviously amused. So in a few minutes he stepped on the scale again and put in another quarter. The slip came out and said, "Your name is Harry Harrison. You live in Sparta. Your weight has not changed in the past four minutes. You still weight 197 pounds; you are still seventeen pounds overweight. You are still on your way to visit your sister in Macon. The bus to Macon is still late. Have a nice day."

Well, certain that he was the object of some kind of ruse, he was determined to fool the machine. So quickly he ran across the street to a variety store and he bought a pair of Groucho Marx glasses with the nose and moustache; and he bought a black hat and a cane. And with this disguise and walking with a limp, he returned to the station across the street, approached the scale, stepped on, and eagerly dropped in his quarter. When the slip came out it read: "You are still Harry Harrison from Sparta, Georgia. Your weight is still 197 pounds. You are still seventeen pounds overweight. You are still on your way to visit your sister in Macon, but while you were across the street fooling around, you missed the bus. Have a nice day."

The Environmental Sabbath reminds us that while we're fooling around with our machines and expensive and polluting toys and excesses that we really don't need, we're missing the moral bus. And missing *that* bus is very dangerous and life-threatening. So the Environmental Sabbath asks us to get back on schedule by reflecting on our status as co-creators with God and to remember what God's attitude is toward nature. After every day's creation the Bible comments on God contemplating the handiwork: "And God saw that it was good." What God calls good we must not despise. What God calls good we must reverence. What God calls good that has been abused, we must reclaim.

21

✛

The Desert Experience

(Luke 3:1-6)

Today's gospel has such a majestic opening. It's like the prelude to a great symphony. You can hear it just roll along: "... the fifteenth year of the rule of Tiberias Caesar, when Pontius Pilate was procurator of Judea...." That would be in the Christian calendar which came several centuries later, about the year 300 A.D. Tiberias would be the son, the heir and murderous, psychotic offspring of Augustus, whom you remember from *I, Claudius*. Augustus was the good guy, and it was during his reign that Jesus was born.

But go back and listen to that opening and listen to its resonance: "In the fifteenth year of the rule of Tiberias Caesar, when Pontius Pilate was governor of Judea, the word of God was spoken to John, son of Zechariah, in the desert."

In the fifth year of the rule of Ronald Reagan, president of the United States, when Thomas Kean was governor of New Jersey, the word of the Lord was spoken to Terry Anderson, brother of Peggy Fay, in the desert.

Do you realize that John, son of Zechariah, and Terry, brother of Peggy Fay, were not that far apart, that they shared the

---

same desert? Do you realize that both of them had what is called, both actually and symbolically, the desert experience?

Think for a moment of the people you know who had the desert experience. There was Moses, Moses the outlaw, the wanderer, the refugee. Where did he meet God? In the desert. The Israelites after him, disobedient and hard-hearted, wandered in the desert for forty years to learn submission to the will of God. David fled for his life, from his own seditious son Absalom, hiding in the desert. When Jesus began his mission, St. Luke says the Spirit led him to the desert. When Saul was knocked off his horse on the way to Damascus, before he would become St. Paul, he spent three years in the Arabian desert. John the Baptist lives in the desert so he can announce the coming Messiah. Mohammed encountered Allah in the desert. Hundreds of thousands of hermits, anchorites, and monks have found wisdom and holiness in the desert.

Why the desert? Because the desert is such a basic, unforgiving place. You are as close to the edge of life and death as you could possibly be. No excess, no luxury, no illusions in the desert, just a total, vast, harsh emptiness. You live in total dependency, from hand to mouth, from day to day. There are no distractions, no television sets, no microwaves, no cars, no nothing. Everything becomes intensely focused on the bare facts of existence, of yourself and of God. There is just you—your utter, complete self and the vast emptiness of the desert. And the challenge the desert offers is this: What will you find there? Will you find God? If not here, then nowhere else.

It was in this experience of utter desolation and dependency that Moses discovered God—as did Jesus and a whole army of holy people who lived life on that edge where grace and humanity meet. Is it any wonder that John the Baptist gave testimony to Jesus here in the desert? It is any wonder that for six and a half years, Terry Anderson, against his will, played John's role? I find it significant that this gospel and Terry Anderson's release should occur so closely.

For Terry Anderson gives testimony—very moving testimony—as many of you saw as you watched him on television at his press conference. He's a fallen away Catholic, living in a common law marriage, but what has happened to him? He says he became a better person during those terrible years that the terrorists stole from him. And when he says "better" and you look into his face and into his eyes, you know it doesn't mean better in the sense of "have a nice day." It means deeper. He lived, experienced, the edge of existence in the desert and, like all the mystics before him, he knows that he can never, never be the same. He mentioned that one of the helps "that got a lot of service" was the Bible and so, like John the Baptist, the word literally came to him in the desert.

What words stand out? Three are prominent. The first word is faith—as it always is when one embarks on the desert experience. He was stripped of everything and found it very painful. But as he said, "My faith kept me from going into despair." The second word is repentance. He says, "I haven't been a very good Catholic. I must turn to God more deeply." The third word is forgiveness. He said, "I don't hate anybody. I'm a Christian and I'm a Catholic and it's really required of me that I forgive, and I intend to do just that." The word of the Lord came to Terry Anderson in the desert. Those words were faith, repentance, and forgiveness. Words of power. Words not likely to be spoken unless he had had the desert experience.

He had help. For him, as you might recollect, there were two significant people. One was Thomas Sutherland, the man to whom he was chained for most of those six and a half years. Picture yourself chained to another human being, morning, noon, and night. But Thomas Sutherland, who was in farm management, taught Terry many things about life, love, and farming. He stretched his mind and freed his spirit. The second significant person was Terry Waite, who came to Beirut to free the hostages and who himself was caught and taken hostage. As Terry Anderson said of him, "He risked his life for me. I can't forget that." All this in the desert.

For you and for me who have not literally been in the desert, the desert experience is an absolute requirement for growth and holiness. There is no other way. And what is that desert experience for us? It means three things. First, it means learning to do with less. All the things the advertisers convince us that we need to be fulfilled human beings are lies, and we know it. More clutters the spirit. Less frees it. Advent is the time to learn to do with less so that we may become more. Getting down more to the bare challenge of existence deepens our dependency on God. We have a better chance of meeting God when we have fewer distractions.

Secondly, the desert experience means solitude. It means prayer. It means stepping out of the fast track with its endless distractions and giving ten or fifteen minutes, a half hour, in prayer to God. We must do this even if nothing happens except that we learn to live in our own desert solitude for one reason only: that we might hear the word of God.

Finally, paradoxically, the desert experience also means company. The desert experience reveals that we too need to be "chained" to someone. Terry Anderson had his Tom Sutherland and Terry Waite. We too need companions to walk with us on the way—and in turn we have to be companion to another. Just as AA has its network, we have to network the Christian life whether it's a spiritual director, a confidant, or a small prayer or Bible study group that meets regularly to reflect on the gospel. We need others to encourage us to go on retreats and days or evenings of recollection, to take on a charitable cause, to temper our own individualism.

Terry Anderson, John the Baptist—both prophets in the desert to whom the word of God came. And both, John in his time and Terry in his, on fire with a new sense of mission. For they have also caught the urgency that fills St. Paul's heart and becomes Advent's proclamation: *"Now* is the acceptable time." Not tomorrow, not next week. The word of the Lord comes *now*.

But beware, beware the message of this story: Satan assembles his junior apprentice devils looking for fresh ideas of how to populate hell. One apprentice raises his hand and suggests, "I have an idea. Tell them there is no God." Satan isn't happy with that. He says sarcastically, "We've tried that, much

as we try to tell people there is no God—we tried it in com-
munist Russia for seventy years for heaven's sake (if you'll
pardon the phrase), but people still understand in the deep recesses of their stupid hearts that there is. So forget it." A second apprentice devil raises his hand and says, "Well, tell them
then there is no hell." Satan says, twitching his tail ominously,
"We've tried that too, dimwit, and it won't work. Sooner or
later people realize that mass murderers cannot wind up in the
same place as Mother Teresa (may her tribe decrease, amen)."
Finally, a third apprentice devil raises his hand and says slowly, "Then tell them—there is no hurry."

And Satan smiled.

22

+

Lambs of God

(John 1:29-34)

Familiarity, of course, does breed contempt. And our familiarity with this Scripture we have heard year after year helps us to miss the impact of what the prophet, John the Baptist, is saying. In reality he is saying something very startling, very novel, although we have become so accustomed to hearing it that it passes over our heads. John is declaring, "Here is the Lamb of God." And then he adds a job description: "who takes away the sins of the world."

Well, there's lots of "sins of the world" in every age and what takes them away according to conventional wisdom—or is supposed to—are mighty programs, powerful reforms, or the threat of dire penalties.

A case in point. In the 1920s the "sin of the world" was alcohol and its attendant evils. To take away this sin the government introduced Prohibition. It would make the country a better place. And so, as you recollect, the plan was to prohibit the sale and use of alcohol not only by law, but by constitutional amendment. The belief was that without alcohol, industry would be more productive, the country would be more prosperous, drunkenness would end, wife-beating would stop, child abuse would disappear, and poverty would be eliminated.

And so the political movement that introduced Prohibition was built around the theme of "Save the Children."And the movement swept over the nation as state after state voted to amend the constitution. And at first alcoholism did go down and productivity did go up and society did benefit. But only at first. Then the bootleggers and the rum runners appeared. The speakeasies took over; the gangsters moved in. There were terrible wars and murders and general mayhem. Graft and corruption became so widespread that the law became a joke. The bootleggers even began to operate in schoolyards, selling to children, and recruiting them to deliver the illegal booze. So the campaign for repeal began and again the slogan was "Let's repeal prohibition to save the children." And then state after state voted that the Eighteenth Amendment should be removed from the United States Constitution and in 1933 Prohibition was repealed. Prohibition, the powerful program to take away the sins of the world, failed.

Communism was to take away the world's sin of poverty and inequality. It came in like a lion—full of roar and blood—but for seventy years the top-ranking "equal" comrades got richer and richer while millions of people were massacred in the drive "to make life better." Communism was a powerful, massive, bureaucratic, atheistic movement with an elaborate spy system, secret police, and censorship that ultimately failed to feed the people either physically or spiritually and so it collapsed.

In the United States, the civil rights movement was to take away the sin of racism and many laws struck a blow for the equality of races, but every day we learn that racism is far from dead. The sexual revolution was to take away the sins of repression and prudery but wound up giving us AIDS, border babies, and a massive abortion industry.

The point is that it is no small thing to come along and proclaim that something or someone would take away the sins of the world. It's been tried before and hasn't worked. John the Baptist, it would seem, is a dreamer like all the rest. But that is to sell John short. He is not an unrealistic dreamer. He comes from the desert, from the prophetic tradition of wisdom, and in that wisdom, unlike all others, he gives us a striking metaphor. Notice what he does *not* say, "Behold the *Lion of* God who takes away the sins of the world," that is, a strong, ferocious leader who could fight and conquer evil by sheer force. Instead John says, "Behold the *Lamb* of God who takes way the sins of the world."

And in this phrase we get something different, the message that self-sacrifice and self-effacement and self-responsibility grounded in faith will take away the sins of the world. It's the meek who will inherit Earth. It's the little lambs—and those lambs of God—the little people of principle, honesty, and integrity who will conquer sin and take it away, not the lions of programs, projects, and processes, as helpful and well-intentioned as they may be. Ultimately the battleground is in the heart and that's where Jesus could shine. John had it right.

Two examples. Recently an article in the paper bemoaned the fact that workers cheat and defraud the country's health insurance system, thereby adding such a considerable burden to an already overtaxed system as to threaten a total collapse that would cause great hardship to millions of people. But more than that; the article consistently pointed out that these cheating workers who sought and collected fraudulent compensations (often with the collusion of doctors and lawyers) did not even think there was anything wrong, unethical, or immoral about what they were doing. And moreover, it was noted that such desensitization was present by far among the young, those under forty; they were the majority of workers who had no conscience at all about the matter. Such fraud for them was a non-issue as far as ethics went. The hurt given to millions by what they were doing simply does not register. Their behavior shocks the health system and shocks the nation's conscience. More laws will, of course, be passed; more prosecutions; more "lion" efforts. But, in the last analysis, it must be the lambs—the parents, teachers, moral heroes—who will take away such a sin of the world of the young adrift with no moral rudder.

Flannery O'Connor in one of her short stories tells of two fourteen-year-old girls who used to spend weekends with their relatives. Well, they're twins and are going through a very hyperactive stage, complete with giggling and secrets. And every now and then they call each other "Temple I" and "Temple II" and go off into peals of hysterical laughter. Finally the aunt demands to know what it's all about, and after much merriment the two girls try to explain. They begin to relate that Sister Perpetua, the oldest nun at the Sisters of Mercy in Mayville, had given them a lecture on what they should do if a young man should...should...and they just couldn't finish. They broke into long and repeated peals of laughter and so had to start all over again. They said that Sister Perpetua said that what they should do if a young man should....and again they broke up. But after much hilarity and giggling they finally managed to finish the sentence, "...if a young man would behave in an ungentlemanly manner with them in the back seat of an automobile." And Sister Perpetua said they were to say, "Stop, sir, I am a temple of the Holy Ghost!" and that would put an end to it.

. The girls thought it was hilarious. The aunt did not. But the story carries a point. The point is that if people—the little ones—have self-respect, if they know they are children of God—temples of the Holy Spirit—and take personal responsibility, they need not rely solely on a massive lionized condom program to guide them. Those lambs with self-worth, self-respect, and personal morality will save the world.

Or, if you want a more contemporary example, recall the fascinating movie *Moonstruck*, that story of a vigorous, even riotous Italian family and their need to love and be loved. The mother of the family, played by Olympia Dukakis, correctly suspects that her husband, Cosmo, is having an affair. And then almost by accident she herself is drawn into what we call a relationship. It's nothing more than sharing a meal with a man who happens to be very nice to her. And he accompanies her home and it's a time when they know that nobody else is in the house and he asks if he can come up. And she answers gently but firmly, "No, no, I know who I am."

That's not the lion roaring "no!" It's the Lamb taking away the sin of the world.

"Behold," said John referring to Jesus, "it's the Lamb of God who will make the difference. One who will go silently to the shearers, turn the other cheek, pray for one's enemies, who will counsel that we give a coat to one who asks for a shirt, and go two miles with the one who sought one mile. This is the Lamb who says, Learn from me for I am meek and humble of heart, who would not call fire down upon the Samaritans, or condemn a fallen woman. This is the Lamb who lays down his life for his friends, whose weakness is our strength."

That's John's message, his bold, novel proclamation. Salvation is not from the society's lions. Salvation is from Christ's lambs.

23

✝

The Persistent Question

(Luke 3:7-14)

The questions we heard in today's gospel, or I should say, the one question that was repeated three times, is not only an ancient question; it's a question that occurs in everyday life, in every age, in everyone's life. There are very few of us who are not perplexed with one thing or another and who do not ask, and ask often, the gospel question, "What ought we to do?" And the fact that this same question was asked three times underscores the old biblical device of showing just how critical the question really is. Just as Peter denied Jesus three times and Jesus asked Peter three times, "Do you love me?" to show that something important was afoot, so, in the deeper recesses of this gospel, three times the same question is asked, "What ought we to do?" emphasizing its critical import, its universal tenor, its basic human challenge.

So I would like to take that question that was asked three times so significantly, and ask it of ourselves in areas that we are concerned with these days, precisely as Christian believers.

The first one that would surely be a question for those of us who are gathered here in the last days of Advent is, "What ought we to do to keep Christ in Christmas?" And that query is more than something borrowed from a billboard slogan. It's a serious question for serious Christians in a highly secularized world where each December season works hard, with great sophistication through a secular media, to de-Christianize the birth of Christ into "Happy Holidays," where we are offered, so to speak, an either-or choice between Jesus Christ and Santa Claus.

What ought we to do? The first thing we might do is not dismiss Santa Claus, but reclaim him, put him back in the Christian tradition. After all, Santa is St. Nicholas, a fourth-century bishop. He was what he was, not in spite of Christ, but *because* of him. The two indisputable facts we know about him are that he was enormously generous to the poor, and that he was very fond of children. It is also known that he had a cascading white beard which was not uncommon those days, and that, being a bishop, he wore the customary bishop's robes which were red and white. So when you see Santa in red and white clothes with a white beard, that is a fairly authentic portrayal of St. Nicholas—although he was much leaner. He did not use reindeer, but he used a donkey and gave, not toys, but food and clothing to those in need. He did it because he believed in the greatest gift of all, Jesus Christ, because he was a baptized Christian, because he tried to live the gospel.

Others over the centuries tried to secularize him. The British called him Father Christmas, the French *Papa Noel*. The Dutch kept his name and called him Saint Nicklaus, which became slurred and blurred into Santa Claus. But whatever they called him, his "first name," so to speak, keeps his Christian connection before us: "Santa," the Latin word for "saint." When we see Santa Claus, we see one who became a Christian saint because he was inspired by the love of God.

What ought we to do? We can remember and tell our children the deeper truths about Santa Claus. We can have Advent wreaths in our homes and pray the prayers at our dinner tables. We could send, and should send, religious Christmas cards. Our homes ought to have a crèche, inside and out, to bear witness to the world that Christmas is not just, to us, a commercialized holiday, but a profound holy day.

"What ought we to do?" is asked a second time. This time the question turns not on how to believe as we just explored, but how to live our beliefs. How are we to act if we believe the God-among-us of Christmas? For a response, let me share with you the true story of an Austrian doctor who revealed why he became a doctor.

He said that as a young man he had been conscripted into the German army invading Russia. One morning, on the outskirts of a village, he said, his unit was summoned to parade by the Commanding Officer. Having told the soldiers to stand at ease, the C.O. said, "This morning we have been ordered to shoot the Jews." And then he went on to ask for volunteers to carry out the orders. Not one soldier stepped forward. The officer, he said, berated them, called them sniveling cowards and every other name in the book. But still, not one soldier stepped forward. So the Commanding Officer tried again, and this time he explained that the volunteers need not shoot the Jews immediately. They could use the Jewish women and steal their valuables and shoot them later. And every soldier stepped forward except three. One, he said, was a Jesuit novice, the second was an actor from Berlin who was a homosexual, and the third was himself.

"When the others came back at the end of the day," he said, "I could not even bear to look at them. I could not even bear to eat in the same mess hall, to live with them. Because I was such an excellent skier," he continued, "I volunteered for the dangerous northern front where I stayed until the end of the war. It was that incident that determined that I would become a doctor and devote myself to healing."

I doubt there is any one of us, in our entire lifetime, who will ever be in circumstances where we will have to make such a heroic decision. And heroic that was. But there's no question that as Christians we are faced with a hundred little decisions every day, to put on or put off, as St. Paul would say, the mind of Christ. Decisions about school, about cheating, about relationships, about fidelity, about business, about sex. Every day we who celebrate Jesus' birthday, who call ourselves Christians, are asked to make these minor heroic decisions that set us apart and make us different. The persistent question comes back a second time to us. We Christians, what ought we to do? The story offers an answer.

Now the third time the question is asked, "What ought we to do?" This time the question is not concerned with belief or specific action, but rather with the everyday "tone" of our lives, or, if you prefer, our spirituality. For a reflection that gives us a context for an answer, here is a very short story that a student wrote entitled "Christmas Solitaire." Here it is in its entirety.

Deborah Foster sat alone in her apartment on 64th Street. Her apartment building was in an old section of town and in desperate need of repair from years of neglect. She sat motionless, gazing at her Christmas tree, or what was supposed to be her tree. She had found the tree two years earlier, behind some boxes in an alley. The tree was artificial, faded, and broken in many places. The ornaments consisted of a few strands of tinsel, a string of colored lights, and a little plastic angel.

Deborah got up and made herself a cup of tea and sat down to a game of solitaire. Solitaire was her hobby. She would play for hours, sometimes forgetting to eat. The cards were bent at the corners and faded from many years of use. After a couple of hours of playing, she stretched, yawned, and took another look at her tree. She studied it closely. Funny, she thought, as she keened her eye on the angel. It seemed to be smiling at her. The way the light reflected off it made it glow, almost filled the room with human warmth. The angel's arms were outstretched as if they wanted to hug Deborah.

She sat back down and listened to the outside noises. And then she heard faint footsteps, gradually getting louder; then some Christmas carols being sung. She saw a handful of change on the table and thought about giving it to the kids. She got up to get the change and stopped herself, thinking, "If I don't make any noise, they'll go away...." She never finished the thought. A loud crash echoed. The angel had fallen off the tree and was shattered. The angel's look was different. She was frowning now.

End of story.

What ought we to do? What ought *we* to do? We are Christians. We carry that name. Three times people asked the prophet John that question. Three times he answered. He said in effect, first, we are to choose Jesus; second, we are not only to live a life but a moral life; third, we are to love. Choose, live, and love are the answers. They are Advent's answers. They are Christmas's answers. They are the Christian answers to the persistent question.

24

+

The Visit

(Luke 1:39-55)

I always feel a certain love-hate relationship with this particular gospel. This gospel has been enshrined in Catholic tradition in what we know as the Visitation. Most of us could probably conjure up pictures of drawings and famous paintings of the meeting of these two women, Mary and Elizabeth. And included in the mental imagery that we have of the Visitation is this: Mary, the perfect flower of God's creation, entertains an angel, learns that she is full of grace, is to become the mother of the Messiah, and in her superb charity runs to her aged cousin Elizabeth to selflessly help her in *her* pregnancy. And so our concept of the Visitation is complete and we have another tableau in the life of Mary.

But the fact is that this is simply piety gone astray, and if we believe *that*, then we lose the whole impact of today's gospel which must be seen in the context of the Annunciation. And when we go back to the Annunciation in the gospels, we see that today's gospel is not a celebration of an angelic visit to a

queen who was kneeling at prayer, but is rather the unexpected breaking into the life of a peasant who very likely
had just taken out the garbage. It's the story of a shrewd and
witty native woman who wanted to check her facts.

After all, remember that the message of the Annunciation
was that both she and Elizabeth would become pregnant.
Mary believes, but still she is a hard-nosed, common-sense
peasant woman, and she would like to have a second opinion.
So what does she do? She puts on her shawl and runs over to
her cousin Elizabeth and before she can ask the delicate question, Elizabeth greets her with, "Blessed are you among wom-
en and blessed is the fruit—the baby—of your womb, and how
is it that the mother of my Lord should come acalling?" And
Mary laughs because she heard what she had come to hear,
namely, "Yes, dearie, we're both pregnant!" And Mary knows
it's true and the peasant girl breaks out in song.

What does she sing about? You heard what she sang about.
She sings about God's subversion. She sings about how God
reverses all plans and designs. God chooses the little instead of
the big, chooses the weak instead of the strong, lifts up the
lowly, puts down the mighty. And God makes fruitful both a
young virgin and an elderly woman. How Mary and Elizabeth
must have laughed and cried and hugged each other and had
a good time. Mary knew! She knew that she was chosen not
because of her purity and goodness—later generations would
get sidetracked into that—but because she was a nothing. She
was a nobody, and *still* God broke into her life.

We sing about Mary's maternity because she deserves it.
Mary sings about it because she *doesn't* deserve it. You see the
point of the gospel? As long as we project Mary as the perfect
woman of queenly stature, then we know it's absolutely right
that she should be the mother of the Messiah, that the break-in
of God's word into her life was completely fitting and totally
to be expected. She is, after all, a quality person. She is holy, a
great saint. And what else would a great saintly woman do but
forget herself and run to take care of her elderly cousin? And
the result of that understanding is that we applaud Mary and

then we go about our business because we certainly are not made of the same stuff as Mary and therefore can expect no breaking-in of God's word into our lives. And Mary weeps over that.

She weeps because we have it all wrong. She did not sing about herself. She sang about God and how God turns everything upside down—for her, for you, and for me. The episode that we call the Visitation says that if God could break into the life of an ignorant, small-town peasant girl, God could and would do it to all lonely, lowly, broken, and insignificant people such as you and me. That's what Mary sang about. She was sounding the note of the mission of Jesus himself. After all, he was born in a stable rather than in the local Holiday Inn. He came and lived in Nazareth, not the capital city of Jerusalem. When he grew up he hob-nobbed with the poor, the destitute, those outside the law. What Mary is singing about is simply that same motif, about how much God has preference for those who are nobodies, like herself. What did she call herself? "Behold, look at the handmaid, the servant, the slave-girl of the Lord—and the one who is mighty has done great things for the likes of me!"

The gospel, therefore, is not the story of the visitation of two reigning queens. It is the telling of the meeting between two bewildered peasant women who are drunk on God's breaking into their insignificant lives. And when we understand that, we open our lives to God as well. Otherwise, if we project that much on Mary, saying that, of course, she was so great and queenly that it would be expected that God would enter her life, but since I am neither great nor regal, I cannot expect that. But that's not what the gospel says. The gospel speaks consistently of the little people being broken into by God's word. And therefore that does not permit us to put God off because we are not qualified. That's what I find wrong with our concept of the the Visitation as we have come to understand it.

It's been a good number of years ago, but you may recall the great, black contralto, Marian Anderson—magnificent woman, magnificent voice—about whom the Broadway impresario Sol

Hurok liked to say that she had not simply grown great, but rather that she had grown great simply. Well, this same Sol Hurok recalls that one day, at the height of her career, reporters asked Marian Anderson to name the greatest moment of her life. Hurok recounts:

> I was in that dressing room when the reporters came in and I was curious to hear the answer. After all, I knew that she had many, many great moments to choose from. There was the night, for example, that Toscanini told Marian Anderson that she had the greatest voice of the century. There was the private concert that she gave at the White House for the Roosevelts and the King of England. There was the time that she got the famous ten-thousand-dollar Bach award from her hometown of Philadelphia. Then, of course, to top it all, there was that famous Easter Sunday in Washington when she stood beneath the statue of Abraham Lincoln and sang for seventy-five thousand people, including members of the Supreme Court, cabinet members, and most members of Congress.

Which of these big moments did she choose? Sol Hurok says she chose none of them. Miss Anderson told the reporters that the greatest moment of her life was the day she went home and told her mother she wouldn't have to take in washing any more.

And that, in a nutshell, is the gospel we heard today. Mary was a washerwoman, a minority figure in an occupied territory, living in the hick town of the time, for Nazareth was a wretched, backwater place. And as Marian Anderson came home one day and told her mom that she wouldn't have to take in washing any more, so God came into Mary's home one day and said she was to be the mother of the Messiah. Marian Anderson's mom and Mary are sisters under the skin. We are therefore celebrating in this gospel today what God did for her, what God can do for you and for me.

When we picture this tableau of the Visitation, we should always remember the song Mary sang about God and make it our song:

He has lifted up the lowly and put down the mighty.

He has given the hungry good things to eat and has deprived the rich.

He who is mighty has done great things for the likes of me and holy is his name.

25

✝

Christmas Passion

(Luke 2:1-14)

Have you ever done what your better judgment said you should not do? Most of us have at one time or another. Well, let me play the "Grinch" tonight and confess that what we did at the opening of our Mass this evening and will do at all the Christmas Masses—namely, have sweet little shepherds install the baby doll Jesus into the manger—was against my better judgment. It was against my better judgment because, touching as it is, it gives the wrong message, which is to focus on the sentimentality of the little baby. And who of us did not nudge our neighbor and whisper, "Isn't that darling? Isn't that cute?" even though, as a matter of record, the baby Jesus has no role in the gospel narrative.

So you say, "Well, what is the right message?" The right message, I repeat, is not a soft, darling baby. The right message is a fierce and a passionate God. The Christmas message and the Christmas celebration is God's great zeal for us, the commitment not to leave us abandoned. It comes down to that: not to leave us in the darkness of political, social, or personal tyrannies. The message of Christmas is summed up in that communication the angel made to Mary at the Annunciation when he made a play on words. He said, You shall call his name Jesus and he shall be nickednamed Emmanuel, which translates "God with us." What you have, then, in Christmas is a terrible desire on God's part to "be with us," to be a part of the human condition: our losses, our recessions, our disappointed and fractured relationships; the deaths we've had in the past year; the difficulties, the addictions, the alcohol, the drugs, sex; things that turn us upside down a great deal. In all of our entire human condition, the Christmas message is that God doesn't want to let us alone but wants to reach out and be with us. God, the most passionate of Lovers, wants to be Emmanuel.

Let me restate this by sharing a true story. The story mentions a baby because it's told by a woman, the baby's mother, but the point of the story lies far beyond the baby. It tells of God's passion for us. Here is this mother's story:

It was Sunday, Christmas. Our family had spent a holiday in San Francisco with my husband's parents, but in order for us to be back at work on Monday, we found ourselves driving the 400 miles back home to Los Angeles on Christmas Day.

We stopped for lunch in King City. The restaurant was nearly empty. We were the only family and ours were the only children.

I heard Erik, my one year old squeal with glee. "Hithere," the two words he always thought were one. "Hithere," and he pounded his fat baby hands—whack, whack, whack—on the metal high chair. His face was alive with excitement, his eyes were wide, gums bared in a toothless grin. He wriggled and giggled, and then I saw the source of his merriment. And my eyes could not take it in all at once.

A tattered rag of a coat, obviously bought by someone else eons ago, dirty, greasy, and worn; baggy pants; spindly body; toes that poked out of would-be shoes; a shirt that had ring-around-the-collar all over; and a face like none other—gums as bare as Erik's.

"Hi there, baby. Hi there, big boy, I see ya, Buster."

My husband and I exchanged a look that was a cross between "What do we do?" and "Poor devil."

Our meal came and the banging and the noise continued. Now the old bum was shouting across the room, "Do you know patty cake? Atta boy. Do you know peek-a-boo? Hey, look! He knows peek-a boo!"

Erik continued to laugh and answer, "Hithere." Every call was echoed. Nobody thought it was cute. The guy was a drunk and a disturbance. I was embarrassed. My husband, Dennis, was humiliated. Even our six year old said, "Why is that old man talking so loud?"

Dennis went to pay the check, imploring me to get Erik and meet him in the parking lot. "Lord, just let me get out of here before he speaks to me or Erik," and I bolted for the door. It soon was obvious that both the Lord and Erik had other plans.

As I drew closer to the man, I turned my back, walking to side-step him and any air that he might be breathing. As I did so, Erik, all the while with his eyes riveted to his best friend, leaned over my arm, reaching with both arms to a baby's pick-me-up position. In a split-second of balancing my baby and turning to counter his weight, I came eye-to-eye with the old man.

Erik was lunging for him, arms spread wide. The bum's eyes both asked and implored, "Would you let me hold your baby?" There was no need for me to answer since Erik propelled himself from my arms to the man. Suddenly a very old man and a very young baby consummated their love relationship.

Erik laid his tiny head upon the man's ragged shoulder. The man's eyes closed and I saw tears hover beneath the lashes. His aged hands, full of grime and pain and hard labor, gently, so gently, cradled my baby's bottom and stroked his back. I stood awestruck.

The old man rocked and cradled Erik in his arms for a moment, and then his eyes opened and set squarely on mine. He said in a firm, commanding voice, "You take care of this baby." And somehow I managed "I will" from a throat that contained a stone.

He pried Erik from his chest, unwillingly, longingly, as though he was in pain. I held my arms open to receive my baby, and again the gentleman addressed me: "God bless you, M'am. You've given me my Christmas gift." I said nothing more than a muttered "thanks."

With Erik in my arms, I ran for the car. Dennis wondered why I was crying and holding Erik so tightly. And why I was saying, "My God, forgive me. Forgive me."

I would like to suggest that the meaning of Christmas is Erik. Erik is God. Erik is Christmas. Erik is God's arms, zeal, and passion for us tattered bums with our tattered lives, our tattered hurts, our tattered relationships, and our tattered sins. Erik is two arms determined to break into our lives.

Erik is a fierce little baby who makes no distinctions but would embrace the least likely. And that's what Christmas is about. It's an enormously unrelenting kind of a feast. It is not sentimentality. It is not soft. It is as hot and hard as any romance. It is God's fulfilled desire to be with us. And that's why we celebrate.

If God is not with us and if God has not embraced our tattered lives, woe is us. There is no hope. And there is no light, only darkness and despair. And we are here tonight out of fruitless hope, pressured routine, or empty sentimentality.

But if we are here because of love and we are here like ragtag shepherds to kneel and rejoice, then we have caught Christmas's meaning: Emmanuel, the passionate God, has had his way and has hugged us fiercely.

26

✝

Who Is That?

(John 15:1-8; Acts 8:26-40)

"Deacon Philip was asleep." So begins a fascinating story in today's first reading, a story that continues and expands the Easter message. Philip's sleep did not last long, because suddenly, as they are wont to do, an angel stands by his side—as did, you recall, an angel in a dream to the sleeping Joseph, espoused to Mary—and awakens Philip. He has a strange message. He tells Philip to go out into the middle of the desert at noon time. Philip does not question it, and betakes himself to the desert and there he meets a man.

Well, perhaps not quite a man, for he is described as a eunuch. A eunuch was a man, who, in a society that prized, above all else, having children, would never have a family. Thus he was an outcast. He was either under a vow or infertile or castrated to keep him obedient and close to the royal court. That might be a possibility because he is described as a chamberlain in the court of the Queen of Ethiopia. He is returning from a visit to the temple in Jerusalem and while he's riding in his chariot he stumbles across a very obscure passage from the fifty-third chapter of Isaiah which catches his eye and stirs up his heart. This was, you recollect, the passage he was reading:

> He was oppressed and he was afflicted,
> yet he did not open his mouth;
> Like a sheep he was led to the slaughter
> and like a lamb silent before its shearer
> so he does not open his mouth.
> In his humiliation justice was denied him.
> Who can imagine his future?
> For he was cut off from the land of the living.

Well, in this passage, whoever the prophet is talking about, there is no future for him, and none could be imagined. For the Israelite this meant no posterity, no children, no grandchildren so that the name would live on. Truly, such a one is cursed, "cut off from the land of the living." He is without family. Who is this forsaken person? Who is this that is so much like the eunuch himself?

And so when Philip climbs into the chariot, that's the first question the eunuch asks Philip. Who is that? Who is that? Is the prophet talking about himself or someone else? The eunuch is agitated. Why? Why is he so interested in this obscure though beautiful passage?

It's because he identifies with it. He is a eunuch and he knows very well that in his ancestral Scripture, in Deuteronomy 23, it says very plainly—and I quote: "The eunuch shall *not* have a place in the assembly of the Lord." There's no place for the likes of him. This sexless person will never have his own family and will therefore have no place in God's family. He can never go to the Temple and praise God with the rest of those who are blessed with children. He too is forsaken.

And so the eunuch, reading the passage, wants to know, who is this cut off like himself? Who is this, cut off, like himself, from the land of the living, without posterity, without children, without family, and therefore without a future? He wants to know because, as he continued to read further in Isaiah, he discovered a note of hope concerning this hapless figure, for Isaiah had continued :

> Do not let the foreigner joined to the Lord say,
> "The Lord will surely separate me from his people";
> Do not let the eunuch say, "I am just a dry tree"
> For thus says the Lord:
> To the eunuchs who keep my sabbaths,
> who choose things that please me
> and hold fast to my covenant,
> I will give them, within my house and within my walls,
> a monument and a name
> better than sons and daughters;
> I will give them an everlasting name
> that shall not be cut off.

You see what this passage meant for him? This man had just been down to the Temple at Jerusalem searching the Scriptures trying to find some comfort but found none. He had been to the Temple but they would not let him in because that same Scripture says, "Exclude this man!" But, now, on the way home, he has discovered a passage in that same Scripture that offers hope and acceptance and community. He has found someone else "cut off from the land of the living," and who could imagine no future but who nevertheless was given promise, a monument, and an everlasting name.

So who is this, the eunuch wants to know, and he asks Deacon Philip. "Why," answers Philip, "that is Jesus of Nazareth he is referring to. Jesus of Nazareth was like you. He too was cut off by choice. He had no family. He had no issue. He had no posterity. And yet he created the largest family in the world. The Good News is that the day has arrived when the excluded one is included." "Really? And am I included?" "Of course," answers Philip. And so, as we heard, right then and there, in the desert, a white man and a black man, a Palestinian Jew and an Ethiopian Arab went toward the water. Philip baptized the eunuch. In this new family, water is thicker than blood.

And that's the thrust of the Scriptures today. No one is to be cut off. All branches are grafted onto Christ. The family of Jesus is not to be exclusive, but inclusive. Those cut off, those who are different, are welcomed into the assembly. This hope, this yearning, this Good News, would find endless variations in the hearts and stories of people, especially the disenfranchised.

The slaves on the plantation on the shores of Virginia in 1830 had just such an idea of their Savior. He would come, they said and sang, from Granada and he would be—a mulatto! He would be part white and part black. And not only that, but the slaves prayed to God to save both them *and* their white owners, the white folk who lived in the big house on the hill; the white folk who whipped them, abused them, and chained their ankles even when they went to church. They had a concern for their white masters and they looked forward to a new world where there would be no owners and no slaves but one family from which no one would be excluded, no one cut off.

There is a priest, a missionary from the 1940s who had been expelled from China. On his way home he got passage to India and from India he was going back to the States. While he was laying over in India he found a huge coastal strip where there were refugees of a community of Jews who had fled the Nazi persecution. There was no effort to help or accept them. They lived in attics and barns throughout the city. It was near Christmas time, so Father Goldry sold his boat ticket and instead brought the Jews pastries so they could celebrate Chanukkah. He then wired for more money to get back to the States. When he got back, his superior scolded him. "Why did you do that? These Jews don't believe in Jesus." He replied, "But I do."

Who is this? Who is this who would do such a thing and give such an answer? One who follows Jesus.

Once there was a very handsome, blond, fair, blue-eyed young man, talented and popular but who, to no one's knowledge, had great interior suffering. The reason for it was that he was carrying a heavy guilt. He had betrayed his dark and handicapped brother. To distract his mind he travels the world and stops off in Palestine. And in Palestine he visits the little town of Emmaus where, he remembers, Jesus appeared to the disciples. And at Emmaus he has a vision of Jesus, alive and strong and radiant. And all of his apostles come rushing toward him and Jesus laughs as he gathers them and embraces them. But all of a sudden Jesus becomes very agitated, drops his arms, and looks around and exclaims, "One of you is missing. Ah," he says,"I know! Judas! Where's Judas?" "Here I am!" cries the young man, anguished and horrified to hear the words coming out of his own mouth. He comes out of the shadows and falls at the feet of Jesus. Jesus lifts him up and embraces him and kisses him and says, "Oh, beloved Judas, I could never have done it without you."

Who is that? Who is that who would not exclude even Judas? Who would accept people who are—different? "Who is that," the eunuch wanted to know, "who would accept people like me, who makes no distinction between race or sex or position? Who can help me imagine a future?" And Philip says, "Why, it's Jesus of Nazareth."

And the Scripture demands that we add, "And those who follow him."

27

✝

A Homily for
a Long Time Dying

(Mark 15:33-39; 16:1-6)

Before Carol died, she asked me to preach her homily. She said she didn't want a eulogy. I said she was right; eulogies were for family and friends to give. The homilist must break open the word of God. Were I to preach, that's what I hoped to do. So the time has come and here I am.

Finding a word to break open was, in fact, easy, especially at this time of the year. It was easy to know instinctively what Scripture to pick: what else but, as you heard, the passion narrative from the gospel of Mark.

Of the four accounts of the death of Jesus, Mark's is the starkest. He gives us a picture of Jesus being systematically stripped away of everything: clothes, friends, blood, dignity, consolation, life itself. Stripped little by little, hour after hour, till nothing was left. Total abandonment.

There's both a legend and a tradition connected with Mark's

account. The *legend* says that the stripping took so long—the torture, the carrying of the cross, the crucifixion, the horrible three-hour agony, the long dying—that Jesus knew the pain it was causing so many, especially his mother. So at the end of the three hours, he searched out her eyes to ask permission to die. She nodded her head and then, satisfied, he let out his cry, his last words, "It is finished!"

The *tradition* says that he was then taken down from the cross, from his bed of pain, and placed in the arms of that same mother. And so we have the *Pieta*—humanity embracing its dreaded enemy, death, and wondering if this is all there is. Finally, however, Mary too had to repeat her Son's words, "It is finished," and let him go. She had to let others take him and put him away, out of sight. And the moment he was laid in the tomb and the stone rolled in place, the legend and the tradition converge to say that a strange thing happened: both Jesus in the tomb and Mary without—and all the others who were there—in a kind of Greek chorus shouted together with relief, It *is* finished! It is finished!

> They had watched so long,
> cried so often,
> comforted so frequently,
> agonized so deeply,
> journeyed so far,
> prayed so hard,
> spoken so much,

until they were exhausted. Until death just *had* to be, because behind its release was blessed peace. For Jesus. For Mary. For friends. For all on that hill of Calvary.

It is finished. But, as they were to learn, not quite.

* * * *

What a remarkably personal gospel for Carol and her family! How it fits!

First, like Jesus, for Carol too everything was slowly

stripped away. Two years of operations, sickness, incapacity...loss. Loss of legs, movements, motion, family, parish—and *control*, the hardest of all!

Secondly, for two years her family watched, suffered, comforted, journeyed, prayed, and prepared—until they recognized that, on their hospital hill of Calvary, death *had* to be.

There came a point when Carol and Denis—and her children and her friends—had to search out each other's eyes and nod permission to die. And I too, like one born out of due time, about ten days ago, had a chance to be with Carol. In that half hour I told her she had fought the good fight ("Damn right!" she answered) and added, "If you want to go somewhere else, it's O.K."

Her bravado dropped. She understood. She had gotten permission. She mulled it over, accepted it, and finally, last Tuesday evening, she died. It is finished.

And, then, finally, blessed relief. She had let go. They had let go. And, finally, at this community liturgy, we too let go. Like Mary, we cradle Carol in our collective arms for the last time and then let her go.

It is finished. But not quite, any more than it was on Calvary. Like the people on that hill, we are now assaulted by our emotions: mourning, grief, anger, guilt, emptiness—but, finally, hope.

Because, in the Jesus story, something else happened. It wasn't quite finished. At the moment of his total emptiness, Mark's gospel suggests, Jesus was raised up to a new life. Like the seed which in *its* moment of death begins to sprout, so was it for Jesus. The grave was his seeding place. The love of God was too strong. Death could not hold him. And so there was resurrection. The Good News is that, since Calvary, death is no longer the last word. It is the next to the last word. The last word is life. Life given, life given to Carol and, as Jesus promised, given abundantly.

Our symbols proclaim such Good News: the Paschal Candle is Christ the Light overcoming the dark-tombness of death. The baptismal robe on her coffin is a sign of new birth. The flowers and song denote the undercurrent of hopeful joy as we grieve. And, above all, the Risen Christ who no longer says, "It is finished," but who says, "I am the resurrection and the life. The one who believes in me shall live forever."

In a word, the message is that God's love is stronger than death and that Carol, who so much could identify with this gospel, with all that went on at Calvary, can and does enjoy that life forever. The door of death that slammed on her when all was finished has opened up to the arms of a God who has always loved her. As the poet says,

Is there a leaf upon the tree
The Father does not see?
Leaves fall, so do we all
Return to earth, to sod.

Sparrows and kings,
And all manner of things
Fall, fall into the hands
Of the Living God.

Carol, the journey is over. That long, hard journey.
Carol, you are relieved. We are relieved.
Carol, it is finished.
Carol, by the grace of God, it is just beginning!

28

✛

Homily for a Cancer Victim

(John 11:32-45)

The gospel story you just heard contains four principal characters, who not unamazingly resemble the four types of people who have gathered here this morning in church. I say "not unamazingly" because people of every age have had to come to terms with our most dreaded enemy, death, and this included the early Christian communities.

Such communities knew, for example, the death, the terrible and premature death, of their leader. They knew the deaths of their relatives and friends. And to try to make sense of it all, they searched their memories and finally recalled stories like you just heard, and they wrote them down and preserved them so that people like us, some two thousand years later, could get behind and into the story and find hope for our despair and comfort for our grief, just as they did. So let's look at that story anew because, when all is said and done, it is our story today.

The first character, the one who is the reason for the story, is a man named Lazarus. He is described as being bound, slowly and methodically, round and round, in those linen strips like a mummy, which was the custom of burial in those days. It doesn't take too much of a leap in imagination to substitute Bob Tweeddale for Lazarus, because those who watched his very swift and terrible sickness saw him every day getting bound with one more strip. Slowly and methodically he became confined. He was bound by his illness, bound by the hospital, bound by the intravenous, bound by the medication, bound by the wheelchair, bound by the sickbed, bound by his bedroom—and finally, bound by death. Each week you could see the strips, so to speak, rapidly going round and round his mind and body until he was quite immobilized, quite still. And, finally, like Lazarus in the tomb, quite dead. Lazarus and Bob: the same person, bound in the unbreakable strips of sickness and death.

The second character or group of characters who appear in the gospel story—and our personal story—are the people who love Lazarus: his sisters, Martha and Mary; relatives, friends, and neighbors and co-workers, like some of you here. Martha and Mary represent all those who ministered to Bob these past months, particularly his family. Giving comfort and hope, wheeling him here and there; bathing him, feeding him, dressing him, visiting him, watching with him, praying with him, and surely, in private, weeping very hard and bitter tears for him. You Marthas and Marys know how hard it's been to minister to your Lazarus. And how, at last, there is an understandable sense of relief because he and you couldn't go any further. But there has been care, there has been service, there has been concern, there has been prayer, and there has been love. Martha and Mary, wearied and grieving, have no regrets.

But now the story introduces a third character who enters the world of Martha and Mary and the bound Lazarus in the tomb. This character is named Jesus. It is interesting how the story introduces him. Not as we would likely do, with the fanfare of a mighty Lord coming down from Mount Olympus, waving a wand. No, significantly, the story introduces Jesus as he really was—a friend.

Not only a friend, but a friend who loved *his* friend. A friend who loved his friend so much that the story goes to great lengths several times to point out that Jesus wept. He moaned. He cried. He felt the deepest emotions. You can just see Jesus standing there, throwing up his arms, tilting back his head and perhaps letting out a loud cry of anguish in the custom of the Mideast. This was his *friend* who was dead. And he cried. And I think that the story wants us to remember Jesus that way: as friend, as friend to Lazarus, as friend to Robert. And he feels deeply what has happened to his friend.

Well, in our tradition we know well enough the beginning of that friendship. You notice that when the coffin was brought in, we placed it touching the baptismal font. We did this to remind ourselves that that's where it all began. That nearly fifty years ago, Robert's mother and father wanted to share the most precious thing they ever could share with their child: their faith. And so somewhere they brought Robert to a church and had him baptized. And in that baptism a bond was formed between Jesus and him. And a pledge was made that Jesus would always be a friend. He would be faithful, even if Robert were not. At baptism, it was declared, "This is my beloved son, my friend." It is significant that Robert ends up where it all began: at the font. Jesus has been faithful. He is here once again. And, as he did over Lazarus, he weeps over Robert.

Finally, there's a fourth set of characters in the story. They are the crowd: sensitive, weeping, caring, supporting, being there, perplexed at death as all of us are. They are you. They are all of you gathered here out of friendship, sympathy, and compassion.

So the cast is in place: Lazarus, Jesus, Martha and Mary, and the crowd. All are weeping. But then the story, as you heard, takes a dramatic turn. Jesus steps forth, prays deeply, calls his friend's name loudly, and as Lazarus stumbles out of the tomb wrapped in his linen strips, Jesus says quietly to the others, "Untie him and set him free!" And awe struck them all.

How the early Christians loved this story! Now they knew that the love of a friend was stronger than death, that the life of a friend was greater than the tomb. The depth and freedom of Jesus' love was liberating and could make all things new again. Jesus had authority over death, an authority rooted in his friendship-love. And we continue to believe that. We continue to believe that this same Jesus has groaned loudly over his friend Robert, loved him no less than Lazarus, and has said to his angels and saints, "Untie him and set him free. Take away the mortality, the cancer, the pain, the intravenous, the hospital, the probing, the needles, the doctors, the medication. Untie him. Let him go. Set him free."

And so, even in our grief, we celebrate this freedom. An undercurrent of spiritual joy runs beneath our mourning because today's gospel has been reenacted. We dare to wear the white vestments reminiscent of weddings. We dare to place flowers before the altar, those harbingers of hope. We dare to bring out the great Paschal Candle, that Easter sign of the Risen Christ, the Christ who dissipates the darkness of the tomb and who cries out everywhere and at all times for his friends, "Untie them and set them free!" Yesterday's gospel is today's Good News.

Still—for us, even as we enter into the story, even as we try to believe that Jesus has untied Robert from death, we are left with the empty tomb. We are the ones left with the grief and the absence and that will hurt for a long time. But, if it would help, I would leave you with an image.

Picture yourself standing on a dock watching a great sailing ship lying silently and quietly for a wind to fill its sails and set it in majestic motion. Finally, a strong wind comes up and all spring into action. The captain shouts orders, the sailors hoist the great sails, the wind catches them with a great puff, and off the ship slowly moves like a giant sea serpent on the waters. But by and by the ship grows smaller and smaller as it eventually becomes but a speck where sky and sea meet on the horizon. Someone on the dock shouts the traditional cry, "There she goes!" and everyone waves goodbye and goes home.

But the question is, "Goes where?" That ship which is just a little dot on our horizon is just as big and mighty, just as laden with cargo and people as it was on the dock. The difference is in us. The difference is that it has merely receded from our sight and disappeared, that's all. But somewhere, as it moves to a foreign shore, that dot, that tiny ship, invisible to us, becomes larger and larger. And there are people on that foreign shore who are about to set up a new cry. They shout, "There she comes!"

Right now we are like those people on our dock. We've seen Robert go. He has moved from the horizon of death, and we remark with great sadness and grief, "There he goes," and know that life will be so empty and painful without him. But I would remind you that the change is in us. Robert is still as large as life and larger than life, for Jesus stands on that other shore with all Robert's deceased friends and relatives who have also been untied. Together they shout, "There he comes!" And as Robert Tweeddale stumbles forth, Jesus steps out to meet him. They instantly recognize one another. Jesus dries his eyes and turns to the crowd and says once more, as he has done so many times before, "Untie him and set him free!" And then he turns to Robert and says, "Welcome home, friend."

29

+

A Time to Remember

(Sirach 3:2-6; 12-14)

Today we speak of what is past and of what is yet to come. We speak this way because it's not only the end of another year and the beginning of a new one, but it's also the end of a decade and the beginning of a new one—one moreover that is leading us to a new millennium. So it's a natural time for us to remember and the magazines and newspapers and television specials are all offering us their reviews of the past year and decade. They're busy remembering the worst and the best movies of the year, the worst and best dressed beautiful people, the worst and the best novels, the worst and the best celebrities, the worst and the best wars, the worst and the best economies, and so on. A phrase from the song "Try to Remember" from *The Fantasticks* catches the mood: "Deep in December, it's nice to remember."

And so, deep in December and in fact at the beginning of January, what do we remember? We tend to screen out the unpleasant things, so we remember the pleasant ones first. I remember an up-and-down time in my own life when, I guess, I was eight or nine years old and my dad took me fishing, which was not particularly his favorite activity. Actually, the site was a small pond near our house, but to me it was like fishing in the Atlantic Ocean.

At that time I kept a little diary—a school project—long since lost, and I remember after that day of fishing I had written, "Great, wonderful day."

A couple of years later I was hurtfully disillusioned when my mother, in a general conversation, happened to remark offhand that my dad, on the day he came home from taking me fishing said to her, "Oh, what a day. It was terrible!" And so I felt kind of let down. But years later I got back up again because I realized that, yes, fishing was not his favorite thing. Yet, although he did not have a great day, he did everything in his human heart to make sure that *I* did. And that put me very much on top again because I knew how much he loved me.

I think that particular memory was resurrected because I happened to see the movie *Parenthood* with Steve Martin. Those of you who saw it remember that he plays Gil, a harried father of three children, two sons and a daughter. One son, Kevin, just doesn't cut it. He doesn't have much self-confidence. His school performance and social life are a mess. Well, this hurts Gil who tries everything in his power to raise his son's self-esteem.

As coach, he assigns Kevin to second base over the objections of his teammates. Kevin keeps muffing all the catches, dropping the balls and causing the team to lose game after game. Kevin becomes more unpopular than ever. And yet, in a crucial game, sheerly by accident, he manages to catch a ball which saves the game for his team. He becomes an instant hero and everyone cheers—and most of all his father who, like a little kid, is rolling on the ground in sheer ecstacy.

Another episode has Gil going to one of Kevin's parties, dressed up like Cowboy Bill and making himself utterly ridiculous just so that his son could have a good time. And then, toward the end of the movie, there is Gil refusing to work late each night at his job, even though that would mean gaining a partnership in the law firm. He refuses because he wants more than anything else to spend time with the son who needs him so badly.

These are memories I cherish because, beneath them, I am aware that they are such powerful images of God: the God who rolls on the ground when we score and even when we don't; the God who does silly things like leaving ninety-nine sheep to look for one that is lost, or who runs down to meet his wayward son, or who prays for those persecuting him. These human memories definitely resonate and evoke something divine. In any case, there's no doubt that our best memories are tied in with the relationships that mean so much to us, including our relationship with God.

Of course at the beginning of a year, if it's proper to remember the past, it's also proper to resolve to make the future better because there were some negatives in the past as well. That's where our New Year's resolutions come in. Well, since our relationships are such key memories, let me suggest ten New Year's resolutions in the form of Ten Commandments for Husbands and Wives, with obvious application for the rest of us.

The first commandment is, Thou shalt not wrap thy husband's sandwiches in magazine articles about a man's responsibility to love his wife.

The second commandment: Thou shalt not leave Scripture verses about submission tied to thy wife's hair dryer.

The third commandment: If thou teachest Sunday School, thou shalt not use thy spouse's shortcomings as lesson illustrations.

The fourth commandment: Compare not thy spouse with the spouse of another, lest thou be likewise compared and found wanting.

The fifth commandment: Thou shalt help with tasks thou thinkest are not thine, lest they become thine alone.

The sixth commandment: Thou shalt not use the excuse "This is just the way I am" to keep from becoming what thou couldst and shouldst be.

The seventh commandment: Thou shalt not say, "You always!" or "You never!" when thou speakest with thy spouse.

The eighth commandment: Thou shall impress upon thy children the strengths and not the weaknesses of thy spouse.

The ninth commandment: Thou shalt spend thy money building memories instead of buying things.

The tenth commandment: Thou shall pray together each day so that thou shalt stay together until thy hair grayeth upon thy heads.

They're pretty good commandments and resolutions. If they're too hard to remember, let me leave you with three simpler ones. Each one begins with the phrase, "Just for today."

Just for today I will strengthen my mind and will learn something useful. I will not be a mental loafer. I will read something that requires effort, thought, and concentration.

Just for today I will be unafraid. Especially I will be unafraid to be happy, to enjoy what is beautiful, to love and to believe that those I love really love me.

Just for today I will have a quiet half hour all by myself; and in this half hour I will give thanks to Almighty God for the abundance that is mine.

I must close with one abundance that will carry me through this New Year, as I hope it will you too. Years ago I was out in California visiting that remarkable giant sequoia forest. The guide who was taking us through the forest remarked that actually the roots of the sequoia are very shallow. That was a surprise to me and the others. How in the world could such gigantic trees stand up with shallow roots? Why, the first wind would knock them over like bowling pins. So I asked the guide about that. He said, "You're right. But, you see, sequoias interconnect their roots and their branches so that when there is a fierce wind they interlock and support each other. That's why they don't fall."

What a lovely image for this congregation, for God's people. Try to remember this as we go together into a New Year.

30

+

Knowing the Enemy by Name

(John 10:11-18)

This familiar, two-thousand-year-old Good Shepherd gospel has a distinctively modern challenge. To catch its impact we have to move our minds back to the shepherding days and the shepherding ways of the Bible. Most people, of course, are familiar with the twenty-third psalm, "The Lord is my Shepherd, I shall not want. He leads me in green pastures....and even though I walk in the valley of death, I will not fear; the Lord is at my side." Even city folk like ourselves can feel the comfort and power of that image.

In Luke's gospel we get the story of the lost sheep and the shepherd who leaves ninety-nine safe ones to seek out the lost one. Not only every shepherd but every common-sensed person knows what a foolish thing that is to do: to leave ninety-nine exposed to danger to rescue one lamb who would be quickly replaced anyway. But it's that very foolishness, the very unthinking passion of God, that is the point of the story. God's ways are not our ways, the psalmist reminds us.

Then Jesus speaks of himself also as the door to the sheep-fold, and the power of that image strikes us when we recall that in Jesus' day the sheep were kept within a stone wall about as high as your pew, but there was an opening for them to go in and out. So there was no door. Instead, at night time, the shepherd himself would lie across the entrance and any marauding wolf would have to get by him. And so, literally he would lay down his life for his sheep. Think about that one: Jesus lying across our doorway!

But today's gospel adds a further intimate touch. Jesus says, "I am the Good Shepherd. I know mine and mine know me." He knows us. By name. There's a relationship. And in our ever-increasing electronic age, that's so significant. We are such a numbered people: checkbook numbers, driver's license numbers, social security numbers, credit card numbers. We're coded and locked into so many unknown commercial and secret computers. We have been reduced to numbers and, in the worst extreme, people in concentration camps like Hitler's had numbers tattooed on their arms. These prisoners were not human beings with names, but faceless, impersonal numbers. It makes it easier to hate and kill numbers or categories. Those Germans, those Jews, those Arabs, those Catholics, those Japs, those blacks—no personal names, only lumped-together categories with no personality. All abstractions. Easy to dismiss. Easy to hate. Easy to kill.

A wise man once remarked, "Don't count the sheep or else they won't thrive." By that he meant that as soon as you make the sheep an abstraction and a number on your computer, then they are no longer individuals; they are no longer unique and so they won't thrive. Any more than we would. Another man comments how easily we, with our passionate twentieth-century love affair with abstract thinking, forget that to make an abstraction out of some part of reality is to take some meaning out of it.

There's an old Talmudic riddle that asks, "Why did the Tower of Babel crumble?" The answer is because the leaders of the project were more interested in the work than they were in the workers. When a brick would fall to the earth and break, the owners would be upset and bewail the loss of a brick. But

when a worker fell to the earth out of exhaustion, they just ignored him and pressed someone else to the task. So God destroyed the tower not because they were trying to reach heav-
en, but because they were more interested in the bricks than
the bricklayers. This is a good story for corporations that look
only to the "bottom line" and dismiss or fire or move people
around as useful or useless pawns in the pursuit of profit.

But it's a good story too because it underscores the basis of
prejudice and racism, rejection, and persecution. And the basis
is this: reducing people to categories, making them abstractions, not knowing their names, not calling them by name. This
depersonalizes them. But the Jesus of today's gospel will have
none of that. He knows his sheep and calls them by name. No
abstractions for him. We matter to him personally. All people
matter to him personally. To overcome prejudice, therefore, is
to learn to see as Jesus sees, to know as he knows, to call as he
calls, to forgive as he forgives. To overcome prejudice is to see
people as individuals with a name and a history, to be more interested in the bricklayers than in the bricks.

Some of you may know the name of Joseph Abdiah, the
founder of the Haifa Symphony Orchestra in Israel. Some
years ago when he was in an Arab village talking with some of
the people, other villagers approached and crowded around
him and shouted, "We are going to kill you." And he asked
them, "Why are you going to kill me?" They responded, "We
have orders to do so. You are a Jew and we are Arabs, and our
leaders have told us to kill any Jew we see." Abdiah realized
that it would be foolish and unavailing to protest or try to escape so he said, "Well, how are you going to kill me?" They
answered, "We're going to take you over to that well there and
throw you down it." So with great dignity Abdiah walked
slowly over to the well, but by the time they reached the well it
was obvious that the mood of the people was changing. They
began to see him, not as a categorized Jew, but as a real human
being who was not hostile to them and who stood before them
courageously awaiting death. So they hesitated throwing him
down the well to die, but, on the other hand, they had to ask

themselves how they could get around his murder which they were obliged to carry out. They finally came up with a solution. They decided to change his category. They decided to make him a Muslim! And so on the spot they said, "We hereby declare you a Muslim!" And they gave him a new name and continued their conversation. Now it was a question not of a category, but of "I know mine and mine know me." They moved him from a category with a label to a person with a name.

One more translation of our gospel of sheep and shepherd. There was an old Indian sheep farmer whose neighbor's dogs were always killing his sheep. It got so bad that he knew he had to do something. As he saw it, he had three options. One, in true American tradition, he could sue; he could bring a lawsuit and take his neighbor to court. His second option was to build a stronger and higher fence so his neighbor's dogs could not get in. But he took a third option. He gave two lambs to his neighbor's children. In due time the lambs grew into sheep and had other sheep and then the neighbor and his children got to see the sheep not as a impersonal herd, but as something warm and fuzzy, something personal with individual traits and a history and names. They soon penned in their dogs.

The Good Shepherd who calls us by name is a good figure to rally around as we teach our children to avoid prejudice and racism and bias of any kind. The Good Shepherd is a good God to pray to for the strength to overcome prejudice. The Good Shepherd is a good revelation of the God who lets it rain on the just and unjust and sends sunshine on the good and evil. The Good Shepherd is the God of Jews and Samaritans and Gentiles, the God of rejects, lepers, and thieves, the God of you, me, and them, the God who knows all of us by name.

31

✝

The Surprises of Pentecost

(Acts 2:1-11)

I suspect that some of you parents can resonate with this story. It seems that it was a day like today, that is, Sunday morning, and a mother hurries into her son's bedroom and speaks agitatedly at the sleeping bundle. "Look," she cries, "it's Sunday. Time to get up. Time to get up and go to church. Get up!" The son mumbles from under the covers, "I don't want to go." "What do you mean, 'I don't want to go'?" responds the mother. "That's silly. Now get up and get dressed and go to church!" He says, "No, I don't want to go and I'll give you two reasons why not." He sits up and bed and continues, "First, I don't like them and second, they don't like me." The mother replies, "Now, that's just plain nonsense. You've got to go to church and I'll give you two reasons why you must. First, you're fifty-one years old and, second, you're the pastor!"

Ah, first surprise, then laughter. Such is the basis of today's feast of Pentecost. Return to the Scripture, to the gospel. The disciples of Jesus were hiding. They were hiding in fear behind closed and locked doors, shutting out the rest of the world which was hostile, persecuting, and terrifying. They felt better huddled together in isolation planning what to do next, where to go. And then, a surprise! Into their isolation Jesus comes. Through closed doors he walks. Past locks he breaks in. Surprise first, surely, but, just as surely, there must have been laughter, at first nervous and hesitating but afterwards long and loud as the impact of their friend's presence sank in. I'm not sure they would have laughed so long and hard had they known what the friend would ask of them, but for the moment, they rejoiced.

What he would ask, of course, was what the mother in our story asked: get out of bed, get out of your isolation and fear, and go to church—to the assembly, to the world, and announce the Good News. They too are quite correct to protest. We don't like them and they don't like us—that's why they were hiding. But the answer they get is this: You're thirty or forty years old and you're the pastors, the shepherds of a needy flock, the bearers of the gospel, the announcers of salvation and forgiveness. You must go. You have a mission.

But since they're scared and unsure, Jesus promises them another surprise. The Spirit, he says, will come at Pentecost and will enable them to do what they cannot do of themselves. What Spirit? The Spirit of wisdom and understanding, the Spirit of love and compassion, the Spirit of passion and courage. And when that promise is fulfilled, the disciples of Jesus in turn surprise others! They run out of their isolation, break open the locks and doors and in the public square—these people who had recently been in hiding full of fear—they speak openly and even speak in tongues so that some of the crowd laughs because they think they're drunk. The disciples don't care. They are laughing too, and they are busy being surprised that five thousand are baptized that very day. And as each page of the Acts of the Apostles turns, the Spirit continues to cause surprises: of cures, courage, martyrdom, and the remarkable spread of the Good News.

That was then. Does it happen now, the surprise of the Spirit? In a cynical age? Let me share a brief synopsis of Mother Teresa's biography. I don't know if you know that originally she joined a community called the Sisters of Loretto, which is a cloistered community that did teaching. To prepare for her task, she, a Yugoslavian, went to Dublin to learn English and from there she was sent to a cloister in India to teach the English-speaking daughters of the rich. That was her call. Her life was laid out.

But in 1947, you might remember, India obtained its independence, but at the price of revolution where Muslims and others split into warring factions. Food supplies were cut off and the school where Mother Teresa was working felt the shortage. How to feed and take care of three hundred girls? So for the first time in fifteen years she was forced to leave the cloister and go out and find food to bring back.

But while she was out there, something happened. She could not help but notice the terrible carnage. There had been some five thousand people killed, some fifteen thousand wounded, and they were visible all over. It was a horrible sight and it spoke to her deeply. She felt something happening to her. She felt the Spirit moving. She realized then and there that she could never go back to the cloister. She felt strongly that the Spirit was calling her to a different and a radical life. So she surprised everyone one day by asking a permission that was unheard of: could she live outside the cloistered community and in the world? Her superiors hesitated, but finally gave her permission to do so as a two-year experiment.

So out into the world she went, but only to discover another surprise. She found out that after the revolution and war were over that the sick and dying were not just a part of those events, but they were in fact everyday events, part of everyday life in the streets of Calcutta. She was stunned. The turning point came one day when she came across a woman whose body, eaten by rats, was lying in the street. She went in search of help, but discovered that there was no hospital. So Mother Teresa rented a little one-room home and got some volunteers to help this poor woman. Soon someone gave her a larger house to work out of as she gathered more unfortunate people from the streets. And from there it began. The needy grew, the space grew, the volunteers grew until eventually she formed her own community, the Missionaries of Charity. By 1970 there were 585 sisters working with the poor and abandoned. By 1985 there were 2400 sisters working not only in Calcutta, but all over the world, including the Bronx and Newark. Recently the sisters opened up a home for the victims of AIDS.

In her biography Mother Teresa speaks of surprise. At her age, time, and place, she remarks, would she, could she, do something different, *be* something different? She was, like the apostles, hiding behind the closed doors of her cloister when the Risen Christ surprised her. He came through the locked doors and breathed his Spirit on her. He called her to a second vocation. Like Mary, she was surprised by the Spirit in a most dramatic way and the world has noticed the difference.

But that's drama and Pentecost invites us to see it as such, for the apostles, for people like Mother Teresa. But for most of us, the surprise of the Spirit is likely to be more gentle and unfolding. The key is to be open to it.

There is an interesting early woodcut that Rembrandt, as a very young artist, did of the Prodigal Son. It shows the Prodigal Son in full face, dressed gorgeously, falling before his father whose face we do not see. The emphasis is on the son. But at the end of his life, when Rembrandt had seen a great deal and had grown in depth and wisdom, he redid that scene. And here, in this mature piece of his old age, we do not see the face of the son at all. All we see is his back. The focus of the picture is now on the father, on *his* face, on his gentleness, holiness, and compassion, every line in his face bespeaking mercy and forgiveness. And then you realize that the picture is not so much a painting of the story of the Prodigal Son as it is the story of the artist himself, a record of his journey. You can see that, in time, the Spirit has worked on his pride. He had learned humility and experienced mercy and so, almost without realizing it, he had changed his focus from the gorgeously dressed son to the humble, wise father, the God of Compassion. The Spirit had entered quietly through the closed doors of his youth and summoned him to be something more. And those who compared the two pictures were surprised.

Today's Scripture remains steady and comforting throughout the ages and we who are here today celebrating a festive Pentecost must remember the cause of our joy: with God, today's feast says, the book is never finished, life is never over, the door is never closed. Slam it in God's face if we will, lock God out by our sins and addictions as we might, hide from God as we wish, cringe with fear as we desire. Put him off as we might, Pentecost says that Jesus will break all the barriers down and breathe a mighty Spirit upon us, the Spirit who forgives, the Spirit who calls, the Spirit who can make a difference.

It is true: From the apostles to Rembrandt to Mother Teresa, the Spirit is full of surprises.

32

+

The Call

(Isaiah 6:1-2, 3-8; Luke 5:1-11)

Today's Scriptures are united to offer us a very simple, yet very profound, reflection.

Go back to that magnificent vision you heard in the first reading. A little background to that vision will help. The man who is the subject of that reading, the prophet Isaiah, lived in the time of one of Israel's greatest kings, a man named King Uzziah. He had come to the throne when he was about six years old and he reigned for about fifty years. And he was a very good king among the many rascals who had ruled over Israel. He was honest. He promoted agriculture. He reinforced the walls of the city. He kept traditional enemies at bay. So he was a good king and one obviously that many people had known all their lives. Well, Uzziah, the beloved king, got leprosy and eventually died.

In this context we meet Isaiah. He is an aristocratic young man. A blueblood from one of the "400 families" of the time. And he is grieving over the king, whom, most likely, he knew because he moved in those circles. And today's Scripture picks up the scene where, in his grief over the dead king, Isaiah had gone to the Temple to pray, much as we would visit a church. And in the Temple he has what we would call a religious experience. He has a vision of God or senses God's presence and God's call. Instinctively he did what Peter would do and what you and I would do: in the presence of God, in the presence of Holiness, his own sinfulness becomes apparent and he cries out, "I am a man of unclean lips!" Notice that Peter says the same thing, "Depart from me, O Lord, for I am a sinful man!"

What is significant in both readings is that the Lord did not obey either command. God did not depart, but called these sinners, a call that cleansed them of their darkness and sin. Symbolically, in Isaiah's case, one of the great Seraphim angels takes a burning coal from the altar of incense and touches Isaiah's lips with it and proclaims, "You are now clean." Now Isaiah is open to hear God's voice, God's call. And the substance of that call is that God asks Isaiah to do something special with his life. The Lord says, "Whom shall I send? Who will go for us?" And to his amazement, Isaiah hears his own voice responding, "Here I am, Lord; send me!"

Now you have to appreciate once more that this was a young man of breeding, a young man with every advantage, destined for a life in the court, a life of culture, a life of luxury, and a life of power. He has this religious experience that God is calling him to something deeper, and he knows his life can never again be the same. He is a changed man, and then and there gives up his privileged life and becomes a fiery prophet for God. And all because he was called to something deeper.

This sort of thing continually surfaces in the biblical lore. Moses is called from being an overseer of Hebrew slaves to lead those very slaves to freedom, and his life was turned upside down. Zacchaeus, upon meeting Jesus, is changed from being a cheat to becoming an honest man, and it cost him. The writer of our second reading today, Saul, upon encountering Christ's call, becomes Paul, Christ's foremost apostle.

And then, finally, in today's gospel, you have the theme repeated. Three young men, two brothers and a friend, are fishing. Their lives could have gone on as Isaiah's could have gone on, but they too, all of a sudden, have a religious experience: the large catch of fish at the Stranger's behest tells them they are in the presence of something more. They immediately protest their sinfulness and are afraid. Jesus says, "Do not be afraid." Henceforth they would no longer catch fish, they would catch people. And, of course, it did exact a price from some of them.

As we listen to these readings on this particular Sunday, we have to open ourselves to their main thrust, which is the truism that life can never remain on dead center. In any kind of life, to be regarded at all as life, it must move. It can only go forward. We can't turn back the clock. To stand still is to die, or at least to miss out on the life that God offers us. We must grow, and to grow means that we must outgrow the past and outgrow the present and move into a *generous* future, a *noble* future, a *holy* future, an *heroic* future, however uncertain that future may be. And we must be willing to pay the price.

Still, we feel unworthy. We feel we can't do it. But the thrust of the Scriptures is to dismiss that defense and insist, nevertheless, that we are called to do something special with our lives. Not merely to be butcher, baker, and candlestick maker, but beyond that as well. But again, like Isaiah and like Peter we cry out, "I'm afraid. I am sinful. I am ungifted. I am not able. I am deprived. I have a horrible background. I can't do it. I can't answer the call!"

In a similar context, let me share with you the lives of two children. The parents of the first child were somewhat mismatched. The father was unemployed for most of his life. The lad's mother was a teacher. He was born in Port Huron, Michigan. He was appraised by his teachers as having an IQ of 81. He was taken out of school after three months, being considered too backward to teach. He did not re-enroll in school until two years later because he had picked up scarlet fever and a respiratory infection. And he was going deaf as a result of his illness. His emotional health was poor. He was stubborn, neurotic, aloof. He liked mechanics. He liked to play with fire and wound up burning down the family house. The only thing said of him was that he liked to tinker and he liked to fool around with trains.

The second child didn't show much promise either. She was a child of an alcoholic father who was quite abusive. The child was sickly and often bedridden. In fact, she was in the hospital more than out of it. She was considered to be erratic, neurotic, withdrawn. She would constantly bite her nails. She had a back brace from a spinal defect. She was homely. She constantly sought attention. She was a daydreamer.

These two certainly were people unlikely to hear any particular call—but they did. And they responded. The little boy, as you might suspect, grew up to be Thomas Edison, one of the greatest inventors the world has ever seen. And that homely little girl grew up to be Eleanor Roosevelt who spent a great deal of her adult life caring for and promoting and helping the underprivileged and deprived of this world. They both heard a call to be something more than what their lives dictated, a call to go beyond the confines of who and what they were.

Sometimes people protest, "I'm set in my ways. When I was younger I had a dream and perhaps even heard a call, but I was too busy to answer and life has passed me by. At any rate, I'm too old at this stage in my life." And once I might have agreed, except that I came across an article, oh, I guess, last year in the *Wall Street Journal*. It was a story about a man named Harry Lipzig. Harry Lipzig is a lawyer and for fifty years had a law firm. He himself didn't practice law; he just ran the shop, did the business end of the firm. Yet he decided at the age of 88 to get out of the office and get into actual practice. The reason behind the move was an interesting case that came to the firm. It was the case of a woman who was suing New York City because a drunken police officer had struck and killed her 71-year-old husband with a patrol car. She argued that the city had deprived her of her husband's future earnings potential. The city argued, understandably, that at the age of 71 he didn't *have* much future earnings potential! They thought they had a pretty clever defense until they realized that the woman's argument about her husband's future earning power was being advanced by an 88-year-old lawyer. The city settled for $1.25 million.

Again, the Scripture comes back and asks these questions: Is God calling you from a too self-indulgent lifestyle to one of helpful concern for people who are less fortunate than yourself? Is God asking you to encourage those who, because of handicaps in their lives, or poverty, struggle with overwhelming odds? Is God calling you, with your wisdom and experience, to teach children? Is God calling you to some generosity of time or some generosity of money?

In other words, at any stage and at any age of our lives, we are always being challenged to be more than what we are. We are being called to outgrow our past and our present. We are reminded that there are untapped dimensions in our lives; that before we die, to be full and integral people, we ought to respond to the call of God. That's what the Scripture is telling us.

I remember reading about a nun in Chicago who is a chaplain in a women's prison. She had received some extra grant money and so she told the prisoners she had three choices of what to do with the money. First, she could hire a lawyer who would help them review their cases and perhaps shorten their jail sentences. Second, she could hire a welder who would teach them how to weld so that they would have some kind of a marketable skill when they got out of jail. Third, she could bring in a painter and a dancer to teach them how to paint and dance. Ninety-five percent of the women voted for the painter and the dancer because, as they said, "they always wanted to express themselves and never had the chance."

The Scripture makes the same offer: seize wealth, fame, material things—or express what is noblest and deepest within you. The point is, the world needs prophets. The world needs those who would not merely catch fish, but catch people in the unconditional love of God. The truth of the matter is that the voice of God comes to us at any stage and age and asks us the question it asked Isaiah, "Whom shall I send? Who will go for me?"

The Scripture prompts us to answer, "Here I am, Lord; send me."

33

✝

Seven Beauties: An Entertainment

Over the years I have learned a couple of things relating to non-church-goers.

First, I have learned that there are many varieties of those who do not go to church. There are those, for example, who relate easily and even jovially to the priest as comfortable non-practitioners. You know: deep down at the bottom, in our skivvies, we're all the same, right, Father? On the other hand, there are those who are somewhat embarrassed and mumble this or that reason for not going—*they* brought up the subject, not I— hoping for some minor or major distracting catastrophe to occur. Then there are those whose nervous looks tell you that you know that they know that you know they never go to church. Well, maybe Christmas and Easter or, as we like to kid, they're here to get ashes and palms: hence the time-honored phrase, "A & P Catholics."

Then you have the belligerent group or the contemptuous group when the subject of church-going arises. The "no-one's-going-to-tell-me-what-to-do" crowd. You know, the independent ones who let out nary a whimper when it was demanded of them that they get a blood test and license in order to get married or drive a car, who are given no choice but to pay taxes, who kowtow to their bosses and obey assiduously every word from the latest media guru who pronounces to them on everything and anything from their diets to their sex lives.

Finally, you have the loud crowd. They proclaim to one and all who will listen that they believe in Jesus—or Buddha or Mao Tse-tung or Shirley McLaine—but have no truck with organized religion, but whose purses and wallets are filled to the brim with union, gas, library, credit, business, club, and privilege cards, signs of their undying allegiance to and belief in the corporation and the Swim & Tennis Clubs, the epitome of rules, exclusions, and high organization.

Yes, there's quite a variety. Secondly, over the years I've learned not only to enjoy such people, but to have fun with them. I kind of go with the flow and take the line of least resistance and give a laid back response. And so, out of this accumulated lazy wisdom, I offer you the following responses to those who care to tell you that they never go to church any more. I call them—both the people and the responses—"Seven Beauties," after the Italian director Lena Wertmuller who years ago put out a marvelous film of the same name.

Beauty number one: "I don't like to go to church because there are hypocrites there." Well, no question about it, Howard, church-going populations have heavy concentrations of those who are shaken up, messed up, fouled up, bent up, and stood up. They are broken and otherwise unenlightened. Hypocrites, spiritual pygmies, professional do-gooders— we've got them all. It's probably much better to maintain your status and your purity by staying home. Go ahead, spend Sundays mending the fence, watching TV, going to the ball game, hanging out down at the tavern. There everybody watches the game and if occasional sad comments come up about the sad state of the world, well, at least nobody's up there in a pulpit suggesting that you do anything about it. Go to church and you're told you have to be willing to get your hands dirty. You have to admit to being in the same boat as everyone else and you have to be ready to help bail out. No, Howard, you're probably better off not going to church.

Beauty number two: "I just don't think I'd get along with the type of folk who go to church. Besides, churches are always having dumb things like open houses, picnics, and pot-luck suppers." Ah, you're absolutely right, Maggie. When you go to church you run the risk of running into people you've been avoiding all week, you know, those "different" people. They might be found there. You see, Maggie, the church has this somewhat mindless notion that different people should come together to form one body, one people: Jews and Greeks, slaves and free, male and female; the ugly and the beautiful, the smart and the stupid, the straight and the crooked, the liberals and the conservatives, the young and the old, the self-righteous and the searching. Somehow the church thinks that if such a strange collection of people can get together under one roof and proclaim that Jesus Christ is Lord, then there may be a possibility, a chance, that it might spill over into the rest of the world. Who knows? It's an interesting thought, don't you think?

And, as for those potluck suppers and picnics and things, you're right there, too, Maggie. Religious folk are always talking fellowship and community and breaking bread together and supporting each other. And those potluck suppers? I agree with you. It's just a way to hide your leftovers and bring them to church. So this togetherness, this mutual support thing, this belonging with those of the same value system can lead to a lot of indigestion and being overweight, besides mutual support and encouragement. You definitely have got to be careful, Maggie.

Beauty number three: "I don't know. Priests seem to me to be a bit weird and I don't like being preached at." You're right on, George. Priests *are* a bit weird. They generally preach poorly and the sermons they give tend to be answers that people no longer have questions for. Listening to priests week after week missing the mark can make you do some desperate things and seek some desperate options. For example, if you're eligible, did you ever think of becoming a priest yourself? *That* might correct the situation. Or you might get into small prayer groups or study groups or go on a retreat to fill up the gaps of things you don't get in church. Or there's even the possibility that you might talk to the priest himself and let him in on the real world so he can preach better sermons.

Beauty number four: "They're always trying to get me to do something in the church!" Mary, truer words were never spoken. Anybody can see that the fool of a pastor can't keep books. He can't do all that counseling by himself. He can't visit all the sick and needy, there are just so many of them. And who in the world will cover all the mistakes that the average pastor makes? Sooner or later, if you want things done right, you're going to have to do them yourself. So I'd stay away, Mary, because you're right. In this enterprise called the church they're always trying to get you to use your God-given talents. I'll let you in on a little secret: I've known some people who have gone to the rectory for a Mass card and they've come out in a daze. They wound up the head of some organization! So you'd better watch out. Caution's the word, Mary.

Beauty number five: "Church people always seem to worry a lot and get involved in things they shouldn't." A sharp observation, Walter. It could drive you up the wall. Church people are always finding sin and discovering needs and getting involved. They're all excited about exploitation and family life, teenage suicides, world hunger, the trillions of dollars spent on defense and not on children, the incessant garbage the media dishes out. It was much better in the old days when the church was just for birth control and against sex and meat on Friday. This getting concerned about community evils and the poor and the outcasts and the marginal can drive you wild. I mean, just because Jesus went overboard, we don't all have to be crazy. Yeah, you'd better stay away, Walter. It can get very upsetting.

Beauty number six: "I don't like people fooling around with my mind. I like to think for myself." True enough, Alice. Perhaps the most dangerous aspect of going to church is that you could easily mess up your mind—if the message gets through at all. We *are* a strange breed. My God, Alice, if you were at church today, you would have heard a terrible gospel, about one-hour workers getting paid the same wages—the *same* wages, mind you!—as twelve-hour workers. It's gross and unfair. You would have had every right to be angry at God for being generous. Then there's that stupidity about being thankful in adversity. Imagine, dying of cancer and you're going to say, "Praise God"? To forgive one's enemies is a bit much, and to give your shirt away to someone who asks for your coat is ridiculous. Forgiving seventy times seven is pathological, I agree. It's all such radical nonsense. You really could get your mind messed up, Alice. Suppose everybody tried to live like that? Why, we would turn the world upside down.

Beauty number seven: "I'm an independent person. I don't need church as one more form of enslavement. I'm independent. I want to be free. Freedom is the name of my game." Well, there's a lot to that, Phil. We all want to be free. After all, we live in a free land, don't we? We have no Pharaoh, no Ayatollah, no military strong men to oppress us. We have a government of our own choosing. We're not slaves. We are free and don't need church.

Of course in our free and prosperous land, for some reason, one out of every five American children lives in poverty. At times we're appalled at the power we've given to our politicians and our routine corruptions, and appalled, too, by the culture we've created. You know, it seems to me, Phil, that if history lasts long enough for archeologists some five hundred or a thousand years from now to dig back into our age, I predict that they're going to be stunned by what they discover. I picture them, with their knapsacks and pith helmets, unearthing the movies and the plays and the television we watched, poring over the books we read, the pornography we sold, the art we created, the kind of black comedy we laughed at, the talk show hosts we gave our allegiance to, and the kind of horrors that fascinated us on the evening news: violence without motive, darkness without escape, sex without love or beauty; the criminal, the monstrous, the demonic, the psychopathic. I picture them staggered to discover what a large variety of enslaving addictions we had to kill our anxieties and the meaninglessness we were told to live by: the television, the pills, the drugs, the alcohol, the sterile, uncommitted sex. I picture them awestruck to discover how obsessed we were with the very madness that destroyed us.

For all the talk of freedom, Phil, we're really captive in a world we built ourselves, which in many ways is a haunted house, a house haunted by the dark spirits we ourselves raised. Our obsession with materialism, the one-up-manship, the bigger the better, the I and the Me and the easily discarded Others before and after birth, before and after vows, before and after commitments. We're free, aren't we? We're not enslaved. The brand names we simply *must* have in order to be accepted, the music we *must* listen to, the politically correct orthodoxy we *must* adhere to, the language we *must* speak, the car we *must* drive, the house we *must* live in, the morals we *must* live by—hurry, hurry! what's the latest directive from Calvin Klein, Geraldo, Donahue, Madison Avenue, and Hollywood? How must I smell, look, dress, talk, and consume today?

Whoops! I'm getting carried away, Phil. I'm sorry. It's just that when you talk about being free I wonder if we realize the enslavement all about us, you and I, that we foster, promote, and mindlessly give in to. And maybe the church, once in a while, *does* have a liberating word that can give our lives back to decency again. And maybe we might find there a faith small as a mustard seed, but still, we have it on the highest authority that it is big enough. So you're right, Phil. You don't want to be enslaved by any church and by any word that might shake you up or challenge you or remind you that, in fact, we are all enslaved to a far deeper degree than we realize and that only God can give us deliverance.

Well, my Seven Beauties, we've had some interesting conversations, enough to keep both of us thinking as we part pleasantly and go our separate ways. I don't know what they're thinking, but I know what *I'm* thinking as I depart. I'm thinking of the story of the family out for a Sunday ride. It was warm and pleasant. Suddenly the two children in the back began to beat their father on the shoulder. "Daddy, Daddy, stop the car! Stop the car! There's a kitten back there on the side of the road!"

The father replies, "So there's a kitten on the side of the road. We're out for a drive."

"But, Daddy, you must stop and pick it up."

"I don't have to stop and pick it up."

"But, Daddy, if you don't, it will die."

"Well, then, it will have to die. We don't have room for another animal. We already have a zoo at our house. No more animals."

"But, Daddy, are you just going to let it die?"

"Be quiet, children. We're just trying to have a pleasant drive."

"We never thought our Daddy would be so mean and cruel as to let a kitten die."

Finally the mother turns to her husband and says, "Dear, you'll have to stop." He turns the car around, returns to the spot, and pulls off to the side of the road. He goes out to pick up the kitten. The poor creature is just skin and bones, sore-eyed and full of fleas; but when he reaches down to pick it up, with its last bit of energy the kitten bristles, baring tooth and claw. Sssst! He picks up the kitten by the loose skin at the neck, brings it over to the car and says, "Don't touch it; it's probably got leprosy."

When they get to the house the children give the kitten several baths, about a gallon of milk, and intercede, "Can we let it stay in the house just tonight? Tomorrow we'll fix a place in the garage." The father says, "Sure, take my bedroom; the whole house is a zoo." They fix a comfortable bed, fit for a Pharaoh. Several weeks pass. Then one day the father walks in, feels something rub against his leg, looks down and there is a cat. He reaches down toward the cat, carefully checking to see that no one is watching. When the cat sees his hand, it does not bare its claws and hiss. Instead it arches its back to receive a caress. Is that the same cat? No. It's not the same as that frightened, hurt, hissing kitten on the side of the road. Of course not. And you know as well as I what makes the difference.

A long time ago God reached out his hand to bless me. When he did, I looked at his hand. It was covered with scratches, scratches I had given. Still, he reached out to me. Such is the hand of love. Others told me the same thing about themselves. So we meet together to keep reminding each other and to retell the story. I guess you might say we form a community that remembers—and celebrates.

That's my story of why I am a church-goer. Of all the beauties, that might be the most beautiful.

Notes

Preface
If you want a theoretical basis for the connection between story and Scripture and doctrine, see the works of Amos Wilder, Stanley Hauerwas, Sam Keen, John Dunne, and others, including my own *Storytelling: Faith and Imagination* (Mystic, Conn.: Twenty-Third Publications, sixth printing, 1986) and the wonderful Ch. Four ("Ignatian Contemplation: The Use of Imagination in Prayer," by William A. Barry, S.J.) and Ch. Five ("Prayer and the Stories We Use to Imagine Our Lives" by J. A. Appleyard, S.J.) found in *A Hunger for God*, edited by William A. Barry, S.J. and Kerry A. Maloney (Kansas City: Sheed and Ward, 1991).

Homily 2: Sowing the Seed
The Josephine story is from Rev. Joseph Nolan who publishes a fine and challenging homily service called Good News (Liturgical Publications, Inc., 2875 St. James Drive, New Berlin, WI 53151). His insights are frequently different and captivating, and I will often pick them up and run with them. Of course, though he is responsible for some of the insights, he is not responsible for the product.

Homily 4: Coming and Going
There's hardly anyone in the congregation who doesn't know a former Catholic, often as not someone in their own families. Exposed to the media's overemphasis of equating the church almost solely with the (repressive) hierarchy, people seldom

get beyond the head concept of People of God. This is an attempt to propose for the heart some reasons for staying, in the witnessing of real people who are the church.

Homily 7: Rejoice Sunday
The opening story, told with a straight face, brought loud laughter. It is funny and it's a joy to hear laughter in church. But it sets them up for the message.

Homily 8: Advertising for God
Imagine how unnerving to be preaching and spot Edward Schillebeeckx sitting there in the congregation! He had relatives in the parish and used to come to Mass when he was here. It was later that I heard this story about him.

Homily 9: The Failed Parent
The particular "Desert Storm" war of 1991 (an immoral one in my opinion with terrible continuing aftermath to the civilian population; see Raymond A. Schroth's article in the *National Catholic Reporter*, January 31, 1991, page 16 ff.) was the occasion to focus on universal underlying issues. Even as its memory recedes, the larger message in the first part of this homily is worth noting and remembering—and the people were grateful for the reminder. The second part comforted some in the congregation.

Homily 12: The Scribe
The insight is Joe Nolan's.

Homily 16: Love of Self
The Sister Hobday story appeared in *Praying* magazine (P.O. Box 419335, Kansas City, MO 64141). Reprinted with permission.

Homily 17: The Mother-in-Law Restoration
The opening paragraphs represent another Joe Nolan insight; the rest is culled from an article in *Weavings*, A Journal of the

Christian Spiritual Life (The Upper Room, 1908 Grove Avenue, Nashville TN 37202).

Homily 20: The Environmental Sabbath
Not a "storytelling" homily, but one we offered in connection with our annual Environmental Sabbath celebration, a concept originated by Dr. John Kirk, advisor to the United Nations.

Homily 21: The Desert Experience
The release of hostage Terry Anderson after six and a half years in jail in 1992 was a cause for joy—and an opportunity for a communal reflection on the whole experience. The comparison to the gospel was timely and irresistible. To speak aloud the ancient majestic rhythms of: "In the fifteenth year of the rule of Tiberius Caesar..." and then immediately to speak the parallel, "In the fifth year of the rule of Ronald Reagan..." was impressive.

Homily 23: The Persistent Question
For greater impact I've included a longer version found in the gospel, but not in the lectionary selection.

Homily 24: The Visit
Again, a startling insight from Joe Nolan, and appreciated by many of the people, especially the women who felt Mary was too much on the pedestal to identify with her spiritually. For the purposes of the homily I used the longer gospel version that includes the *Magnificat*, which the lectionary strangely omits.

Homily 25: Christmas Passion
A Joe Nolan insight. The wonderful story is from the hand of Nancy L. Dahlberg.

Homily 26: Who Is That?
The insights are from the homily notes of noted author and professor of Christian ministry at Duke University Chapel in

North Carolina, William H. Willimon. They are found in a new and excellent ecumenical preaching magazine, *The Living Pulpit* (President, the masterful homilist, Walter Burghardt, S.J., 5000 Independence Ave, Bronx, NY 10471). Willimon got a few verses mislocated in Isaiah but the notes are provocative and I have fleshed them out here (January-February 1992, p. 40). For a deeper look at this same theme, see the book of Robert J. Karris, O.F.M., *Jesus and the Marginalized in John's Gospel* (Collegeville, Minn.: Liturgical Press, 1990, pp. 105-107).

Homilies 27 and 29: For funerals
These are familiar texts parsed for the empathetic and mixed congregation present at every funeral.

Homily 31: The Surprises of Pentecost
The reference, of course, is to the Bronx, New York, and Newark, New Jersey.

Homily 33 : Seven Beauties: An Entertainment
No Scripture source here, just a longish fun homily saved for last. Used on a blah day. No heavy message, just a light (affirming) point for the congregation. I recall culling this from somewhere many years ago, but have lost the memory of that source. The story at the end is from Fred Craddock from his sermon, "Praying Through Clenched Teeth" in *The Twentieth Century Pulpit*, Volume II (Nashville: Abingdon).

FROM
MORE TELLING STORIES,
COMPELLING STORIES

Lectionary References

1 Decide   Mark 9:38-43, Cycle B, 26th Sunday of the Year

2 Sowing the Seed   Mark 4:26-34, Cycle B, 10th Sunday of the Year

3 Anger   John 2:13-25), Cycle B, 3rdSunday of the Year

4 Coming and Going   John 6:60-69, Cycle B, 21st Sunday of the Year

5 The Weeping Christ   Mark 1:12-15, Cycle B, 1st Sunday of Lent

6 Forgiveness   John 20:19-31, Cycle B, 2nd Sunday after Easter

7 Rejoice Sunday   Philippians 4:4-7, Cycle C, 3rd Sunday of Advent

8 Advertising for God   John 3:14-21, Cycle B, 4th Sunday of Lent

9 The Failed Parent   1 Samuel 2:12-17, Cycle B, 2nd Sunday of the Year

10 Returning — Isaiah 55:6-9, Cycle A, 25th Sunday of the Year

11 Baptism: The Crisis of Identity — Mark 1:7-11, Cycles A, B, C, Baptism of the Lord

12 The Scribe — Mark 12:28-34, Cycle B, 31st Sunday of the Year

13 Slouching Toward Bethlehem — Matthew 2:1-12, Cycles A, B, C, Epiphany

14 The Radical Gospel — Matthew 25:31-46, Cycle A, 34th Sunday of the Year

15 Stewardship — Mark 12:38-44, Cycle B, 32nd Sunday of the Year

16 Love of Self — Mark 12:28-34, Cycle B, 31st Sunday of the Year

17 The Mother-in-Law's Restoration — Mark 1:29-39, Cycle B, 5th Sunday of the Year

18 Decision Time — John 12:20-33, Cycle B, 5th Sunday of the Year

19 Cross, Crown, and Commitment — Mark 10:35-45, Cycle B, 29th Sunday of the Year

20 The Environmental Sabbath — Matthew 6:25-29

21 The Desert Experience — Luke 3:1-6, Cycle C, 2nd Sunday of Advent

22 Lambs of God — John 1:29-34, Cycle A, 2nd Sunday of the Year

23 The Persistent
    Question

Luke 3:7-14, Cycle C, 2nd Sunday of
Advent

24 The Visit

Luke 1:39 -55, Cycle C, 4th Sunday of
Advent

25 Christmas Passion

Luke 2:1-14, Cycles A, B, C, Christmas

26 Who Is That?

Acts 8:26-40, Cycle B, 5th Sunday of
Easter

27 A Homily for a
    Long Time Dying

Mark 15:33-39; 16: 1-56, Funeral Mass

28 Homily for a
    Cancer Victim

John 11:32-45, Funeral Mass

29 A Time to
    Remember

Sirach 3:2-6; 12-14, Cycles A, B, C,
Sunday in the Octave of Christmas

30 Knowing the
    Enemy by Name

John 10:11-18, Cycle B, 4th Sunday of
Easter

31 The Surprises of
    the Pentecost

Acts 2:1-11, Cycles A, B, C, Pentecost

32 The Call

Luke 5:1-11; Isaiah 6: 1-12, 3-8, Cycle
C, 5th Sunday of the Year

33 Seven Beauties:
    An Entertainment

FROM
TIMELY HOMILIES

Lectionary References

1 Prayer

Luke 11:1–13, Cycle C, 17th Sunday of the Year

2 Body of Christ

Matthew 26:17–30, Weekdays 1 & 2, Wednesday of Holy Week

3 Choose

John 6:66–67, Cycle B, 21st Sunday of the Year

4 Forgiving—
    Being Forgiven

Matthew 18:21–35, Cycle A, 24th Sunday of the Year

5 Transfiguration:
    The Lesson

Luke 9:28–36, Cycle C, 2nd Sunday of Lent

6 Good Samaritan

Luke 10:30–37, Cycle C, 15th Sunday of the Year

7 Central Park

John 17:20–25, Cycle C, 7th Sunday after Easter

8 The Persistence
    of Mary

Luke 8:19–21, Cycle C, 2nd Sunday of Lent

9 Trinity: A Matter
    of Relationship

Matthew 28:16–20, Cycles A, B, C, Feast of Ascension

10 Love Trusts

Matthew 11:25–30, Cycle A, 14th Sunday of the Year

11 The Gestures   Luke 7:11–17, Cycle C, 10th Sunday of
    of Hope   the Year

12 Under the   1 Kings 19:1–9, Cycle B, 19th Sunday
    Broom Tree   of the Year

13 Shadows: Luke 7:36–50, Weekday 1 & 2,
    Father's Day   Tuesday of the 24th Week of the Year

14 What Are   Luke 3:1–19, Cycle C, 3rd Sunday of
    We To Do?   Advent

15 Designer Worth   Matthew 6:25–34, Cycle A, 8th Sunday
                                of the Year

16 Radical Saints   Matthew 19:16–22, Weekday 1 & 2,
                                Monday of the 20th Week of the Year.

17 Halloween   Revelation 7:9–17, Cycle C, 4th
                                Sunday of Easter

18 The Cross   Mark 5:25–34, Cycle B, 13th Sunday of
    That Shapes Us   the Year

19 No More Wine   John 2:1–11, Cycle C, 2nd Sunday of
                                the Year

20 Freeing the Voice   Mark 7:31–38, Cycle B, 23rd Sunday of
                                the Year

21 All Saints   Revelation 7:1–8, Cycle C, 4th Sunday
                                of Easter

22 The Good Woman   Luke 18:20–22

23 Companions   1 Kings, 19:1–9, Cycle B, 19th Sunday
                                of the Year

24 Making Wishes Come True — Luke 4:14–19, Cycle C, 3rd Sunday of the Year

25 Taking Up — Matthew 16:21–28, Cycle A, 22nd Sunday of the Year

26 Peace — Luke 10:1–12, Cycle C, 14th Sunday of the Year

27 Holy Thursday — John 13:1–17, Cycles A, B, C, Holy Thursday

28 Abraham & Sarah: A Golden Jubilee — Genesis 18:1–10, Cycle C, 16th Sunday of the Year

29 A Wedding Homily — John 6:60–68, Cycle B, 21st Sunday of the Year

30 A Funeral Homily — Luke 24:13–35, Cycles A, B, C, Easter Sunday

FROM
TELLING STORIES,
COMPELLING STORIES

Lectionary References

1 Be Open

Mark 7:31–37, Cycle B, 23rd
Sunday of the Year

2 Ananias: The
    Missing Ingredient

Acts 9:1–20, Friday of the 3rd
Week of Easter

3 Bartimaeus

Mark 10:46–52, Cycle B, 30th
Sunday of the Year

4 The Prodigal Son

Luke 15:11–32, Cycle C, 4th
Sunday of Lent

5 Zacchaeus

Luke 19:1–10, 31st Sunday of the
Year

6 Naaman:
    A Different Way

2 Kings 5:1–26, Cycle A, 28th
Sunday of the Year

7 John: The
    Disquieting Prophet

Matthew 3:1–12, Cycle A, 2nd
Sunday of Advent

8 Pride as Hypocrisy

Matthew 23:1–12, Cycle A, 31st
Sunday of the Year

9 Capital Sins

Luke 19:45–48, Cycle C, 3rd
Sunday of Lent

10 Weeds and Wheat — Matthew 13:24–30, Cycle A, 16th Sunday of the Year

11 Silence — Matthew 22:1–14, Cycle A, 28th Sunday of the Year

12 Christmas Music — Luke 2:8–20, Cycles A, B, C, Christmas Midnight Mass

13 Epiphany — Matthew 2:1–12, Cycles A, B, C, Epiphany

14 Counterculture — John 15:1–8, Cycle B, 5th Sunday of Easter

15 New Year's Resolutions — Matthew 3:13–17, Cycle A, Baptism of the Lord

16 Five Things Prayer Is Not — Matthew 6:7–15, Tuesday of 1st Week of Lent

17 Between Loss and Promise — Acts 1:1–14, Cycles A, B, C, Ascension

18 Jesus, Collector of the Unwanted: All Saints Day — Revelation 7:14–17, Cycle C, 4th Sunday of Easter

19 Responding to Evil — Matthew 13:24–43, Cycle A, 16th Sunday of the Year

20 My Enemy, the Church — Matthew 5:38–48, Cycle A, 7th Sunday of the Year

21 Caution and the Christ — Matthew 10:32–39, Year 1, Monday after the 15th Sunday of the Year

22 Who Is Thomas's Twin?   John 20:19–31, Cycle A, 2nd
                           Sunday after Easter

23 Not One Stone   Luke 21:1–28, Cycle C, 34th Sun-
     Upon the Other   day of the Year

24 The Great   Matthew 22:34–40, Cycle B, 30th
     Commandment and   Sunday of the Year
     the Retarded

25 Entering Passiontide   John 11:1–45, Cycle A, 5th Sunday
                           of Lent

26 The Meaning   Mark 13:33–37, Cycle C, 1st
     of Advent   Sunday of Advent

27 Lost and Found   1 Timothy 1:12–17, Cycle C, 24th
                           Sunday of the Year

28 Images for the End
     of Summer: Labor Day

29 The Road to Emmaus   Luke 24:1–35, Cycle A, 3rd
                           Sunday of Easter

30 Untie Him   John 11:1–44, Cycle A, 5th Sunday
                           of Lent

31 Holy Thursday   John 13:1–17, Cycles A, B, C

32 Easter   John 20:1–18, Cycle A, Easter
                           Sunday

33 A Wedding Homily: 1 Corinthians 13; John 15:9–17
     For Kerry and
     David Saalfrank

34 A Funeral Homily   Mark 16:1–8, Cycle A, Easter Vigil

35 A Funeral Homily: Luke 7:11–17
    A Young Suicide

Other titles by Fr. Bausch

Telling Stories, Compelling Stories
35 Stories of People of Grace

Wonderful stories that illuminate the gospels with examples of people living as Christian role-models who witness to the effects of being touched and transformed by God.   0-89622-456-2, 200 pp, $9.95 (C-44)

The Word In and Out of Season
Homilies for Preachers, Reflections for Seekers

The 60 homilies herein—divided according to liturgical seasons, feasts, and celebrations, with a section on Parables and on Lessons from Scripture—are presented to preachers as aids, thought-starters, or outright models. Seekers will find here a source of nourishment for their spiritual life. Witty, touching, full of humanity and wisdom.   1-58595-003-3, 304 pp, $14.95 (J-44)

A World of Stories for Preachers and Teachers
*and all who love stories that move and challenge

These newest tales (over 350!) aim to nudge, provoke, and stimulate the reader and listener to resonate with the human condition, as did the stories of Jesus. This book should be in the hands of every preacher, storyteller, teacher, and reader.   0-89622-919-X, 534 pp, $29.95 (B-92)

The Best of Bausch

Here is a user-friendly CD-Rom that has all of Fr. Bausch's stories under one roof! It offers a resource for homilists and teachers, and spiritual reflection for any individual. This CD-Rom includes every Sunday of the 3-year cycle. The stories are provided as a resource to be incorporated into personal homilies, class lessons, or reflections on Scripture. Stories can be revised and edited to fit the user's own needs, then printed out. Anyone who preaches, teaches or has any need to use stories will find this inspirational CD-Rom a great time-saver.   1-58595-113-7, $129.95 (A-97)

Available at religious bookstores or from:

TWENTY-THIRD PUBLICATIONS

PO BOX 180 · 185 WILLOW STREET   MYSTIC, CT 06355 · 1-800-321-0411
FAX: 1-800-572-0788   BAYARD   E-MAIL: ttpubs@aol.com

Call for a free catalog